"Speaking of passion...the public reaction to our photo has officially become a viral event. My team seems to think it's the answer to all of our PR issues." Tristan waited a moment.

Nina immediately stiffened and shook her head, jet-black waves shaking gently with the movement. "For you, perhaps. I can't imagine the comments about me would be quite the same."

He slid his phone out of his pocket, drawing up the curated list of comments.

"The fans love us together and the stockholders love when the fans are happy."

She crossed her arms. "So this is why you came here. To ask me to sign up to be a pawn in this...lie?"

"I don't see you as a pawn, Nina. But I expected a true business mind would see this as the golden bargaining opportunity that it is."

"You want to make a deal?"

"Play the paddock romance out until the end of the season and you're free to go."

T0197859

The Fast Track Billionaires' Club

Finding passion at the finish line!

In the elite and glamorous world of motorsport racing, it's not just fast cars that get pulses racing... Especially when three billionaires from the exclusive Falco Racing team come face-to-face with the only women who dare challenge them!

Can former Falco driver Grayson ignore his long-buried desire for the forbidden when he's reunited with his best friend's widow?

Find out in Grayson and Izzy's story

The Bump in Their Forbidden Reunion

What will happen when an argument between Tristan, Falco Racing's notorious playboy owner, and the heiress driving for his team goes viral...and forces them into a romance ruse?

Find out in Tristan and Nina's story

Fast-Track Fiancé

Both available now!

What will champion driver Apollo do when he discovers the consequence of his passionate night with a beautiful stranger?

Find out in Apollo and Astrid's story

Coming soon!

FAST-TRACK FIANCÉ

AMANDA CINELLI

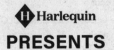

H Harlequin

PRESENTS

Harlequin® PRESENTS™

ISBN-13: 978-1-335-93911-1

Fast-Track Fiancé

For questions and comments about the quality of this book, please contact us at CustomerService@Harlequin.com.

TM and ® are trademarks of Harlequin Enterprises ULC.

 Harlequin Enterprises ULC
22 Adelaide St. West, 41st Floor
Toronto, Ontario M5H 4E3, Canada
www.Harlequin.com

Printed in Lithuania

Recycling programs for this product may not exist in your area.

MIX
Paper | Supporting responsible forestry
FSC® C021394

Amanda Cinelli was born into a large Irish Italian family and raised in the leafy-green suburbs of County Dublin, Ireland. After dabbling in a few different career paths, she finally found her calling as an author upon winning an online writing competition with her first finished novel. With three small daughters at home, she usually spends her days doing school runs, changing diapers and writing romance. She still considers herself unbelievably lucky to be able to call this her day job.

Books by Amanda Cinelli

Harlequin Presents

A Ring to Claim Her Crown

Monteverre Marriages

One Night with the Forbidden Princess
Claiming His Replacement Queen

The Avelar Family Scandals

The Vows He Must Keep
Returning to Claim His Heir

The Greeks' Race to the Altar

Stolen in Her Wedding Gown
The Billionaire's Last-Minute Marriage
Pregnant in the Italian's Palazzo

The Fast Track Billionaires' Club

The Bump in Their Forbidden Reunion

Visit the Author Profile page
at Harlequin.com for more titles.

CHAPTER ONE

Nina Roux kept a polite smile in place until she'd gained a safe distance from the hot overhead lights of the press tent. The rain-soaked paddock of the Elite One Monte Carlo circuit was relatively deserted in the aftermath of yesterday's disastrous race during which ten drivers had crashed. Thankfully there were no significant casualties, with the exception of one career-ending injury for the lead driver of Falco Roux. The team in which she was currently the first reserve driver.

She wasn't so callous as to say she'd been waiting for this moment, but, as a reserve driver, the only chance she'd ever had to get actual race time was at the expense of one of the lead drivers on the team. She had sat patiently during the morning briefing from management, proudly wearing her standard polo shirt and crisply ironed chinos in the team colours of white and maroon. It had seemed straightforward, to promote her into a permanent seat for the remaining seven races of the season. To give her the chance she had earned and one she deserved after graduating top of the academy at eighteen, followed by five years of hard work in testing and development. Much longer than most other drivers had to wait when they performed at her level. Team members had shaken her hand, and she'd felt a sense of bubbling excitement grow within as they'd readied for a 'surprise announcement' that would be delivered during a live-streamed press briefing.

She had imagined how they might announce it. Would they lead with her being the first Roux to earn a seat on their family's team since her brother's ill-fated attempt as a race driver ten years before? Or go with the more shocking fact that she would be the first woman to take a permanent seat in Elite One since her aunt, Lola Roux, had dominated the sport twenty-five years ago?

In the end, they had discussed none of those things... because it had turned out that Nina wasn't the subject of this surprise announcement after all, but rather the signing of a completely new driver. Not only that, but a driver who was the grandson of the owner of their biggest rival team, Accardi Autosport. Apollo Accardi, a championship-winning driver who had stunned the racing world by disappearing from the sport six years ago.

The announcement had come from their new team owner, Tristan Falco, via video link, his handsome tanned face and perfectly coiffed dark blond hair filling the screen as he performed his most basic of duties from somewhere far away. Likely upon one of his famous superyachts, surrounded by glamorous guests and merriment. The potential return to Elite One of the legendary driver had been whispered about all season, and she'd foolishly believed the rumours too good to be true. But Apollo Accardi had indeed made his return, and with it had taken her chance to secure a seat for the rest of the season. She'd get a drive for the next few races, but, once Apollo had arrived and familiarised himself with the car, he'd complete the rest.

As the details of the shocking announcement had been talked through and not one of her teammates had spoken up at the injustice of it all, her chest had tightened with despair and anger. She'd found herself standing suddenly, ignoring the quick warning look from their head of PR as she'd mumbled her excuses and made her exit. Her knees had threatened to buckle with every step she took, cameras flashing wildly to take in her reaction. Watching for the woman they'd nicknamed the ice princess to scowl or tantrum or make a scene that they could gleefully publish on their various websites.

So she'd smiled.

She'd smiled as she'd walked calmly past the line of journalists and through the belly of their impressive track headquarters, only breaking into a run once she'd reached the empty front foyer filled with their legacy of Elite One driver and constructor championship trophies as well as posters and flags in white and maroon. Colours that had been made famous by *her* family name alone for more than half a century until one impulsive playboy billionaire had seemingly swooped in and made her reckless big brother an offer he couldn't refuse. Even when she'd emerged into the rain outside, she hadn't slowed down. Her feet stomped along the tarmac, keeping time with the furious beat of her heart.

She waited until she was a safe distance towards her own secluded motorhome at the edge of the Falco Roux buildings before she released a growl that had been building in her chest. Video link. The biggest disaster that had hit their team in years and their billionaire owner hadn't even bothered to be here in person. Tristan Falco had been almost completely absent from every race and meeting from the moment he had taken the reins from her older brother, Alain.

Famous for his skill in acquisition, rebranding and subsequent big-figure sales of struggling corporations, Tristan Falco likely believed that his usual routine would work just the same here in the pinnacle of motorsport racing. But as evidenced by their recent slide of steadily declining popularity and investments, it was not. She seemed to be the only one willing to tell him why, which she would do if the man weren't utterly impossible to get a meeting with.

If her frustrations with management hadn't already been at boiling point, perhaps she could have held it together today. For any other team, Nina would have been impressed and excited. Nabbing a huge name like Apollo…it likely had cost Falco more than a quarter of their year's budget to achieve. But *she* was the reserve driver, a position she'd held for far longer than any other driver she knew with adequate licence points to drive in Elite One. It was unacceptable. And it was exactly the kind of move that she'd needed in order to make the next difficult decision about her own career.

What was that saying? The definition of insanity was doing the same thing over and over again and expecting a different result. She knew now that there was no other option for her here, not if Falco was prepared to pay an external driver probably triple her salary to come in and learn their car from scratch. The car she had been instrumental in developing alongside the team she'd known from birth. The car she had set their track record in at the end of last year during their winter break. She had taken first place in this year's Legends race, for goodness' sake, after being chosen as a second driver by former Elite One world champion Grayson Koh.

If all of that wasn't enough...nothing ever would be.

It was a gift really—perhaps she had held on too long to familial loyalty. Her charity girls' driving academy was already on the verge of bankruptcy since her shares and inheritance had been lost in the months of financial woes that led to her brother accepting the buyout. She understood why Alain had done it, or at least she had tried to over and over after she'd realised that he had got her inadvertently to sign away every cent in what she'd believed was an effort to save them. Instead, reckless and selfish as he was, Alain had sold their legacy to Falco and left her with nothing. The last she'd heard, he was currently living it up in Ibiza on one of the yachts owned by none other than Tristan Falco himself. Probably another little perk that he'd secured in the secret negotiations that had led to Monaco's oldest and most historic team, Roux Racing, being renamed Falco Roux.

She slammed the door of her private motorhome, turning around just as the door swung inwards. Astrid Lewis, Falco Roux's head of PR, entered, her green eyes sparking with fury behind her designer horn-rimmed glasses. The woman was a silhouette of perfectly coiffed rage and Nina was the sole recipient.

'Before you say anything, I did the right thing by

walking out of there.' Nina turned away, still intent on getting changed and leaving as quickly as possible. The press wouldn't follow her to her late aunt's home in the south of France, and she knew better than to assume she would be left alone if she remained in Monte Carlo any longer.

'Your contract requires you to remain in the press tent for the entirety of each sitting. We just announced a major development in the team line-up following the worst driver injury of the season, Nina.'

Nina bit the inside of her cheek, forcing herself to hold her tongue. She knew better than anyone what happened when she allowed herself to speak freely. Keep calm, she told herself. Calm people didn't lose their jobs. It wasn't that she was unable to control her temper, it was simply that injustice was her biggest trigger. She believed in working hard and reaping a fair reward for her efforts. She *deserved* to be the one in that seat for the remainder of the season instead of just the next few races. She had been the one pushing the team to make upgrades. She had spent hundreds of hours with the engineers during development and they had ended up with the best car they'd had in a decade and were maybe even on track to win a constructor's championship.

She'd put every ounce of herself into being a hardworking team member, believing the results of her talent and drive would be enough. So no, she wasn't going to sit and listen to her team wax lyrical about how excited they were to welcome their new driver to the Falco Roux family. She wouldn't smile and wave and play the good girl a second longer. She had done it for the entirety of her career so far. She had followed every rule and toed every line and look where it had got her.

Superstition and loyalty had led her to sign a ridiculous contract that kept her locked into Falco Roux until she turned twenty-five. But she knew now, she couldn't stay that long. She wouldn't waste two more years in a place that seemed determined to use her and benefit from her talent while giving her none of the recognition or opportunity. Maybe another team would treat her with more respect, give her more actual access to opportunity instead of constantly holding her back with excuse after excuse.

And there was only one man who could set her free.

'I don't like that look in your eye, Nina,' Astrid said warily. 'I know that this might seem unfair, but I promise you there is a plan. Tristan Falco knows what he is doing—'

'Do not mention that man's name in front of me. Not when he hasn't even had the decency to speak to me in person *once* since he took my family's company from under me.'

To her credit, Astrid pursed her lips and remained silent. Good, too, because Nina didn't want to take out her frustrations on the other woman. They might not technically be friends, but Astrid had never steered her wrong in the years since they had both started as newbies on the male-dominated team. Nina as a brand-new test driver, Astrid as a PR assistant.

'Please just tell me what you plan to do.' Astrid sighed wearily. 'And if I need to take measures on my end to counteract any potential damage.'

Just as she'd opened her mouth to offer benign re-assurance, Nina's phone beeped, grabbing her attention. A slow breath escaped her lips as she read the text message. A smile slowly spread across her face as she realised it was exactly the news she'd hoped for. She'd nabbed a last-minute invitation to an exclusive event taking place in Paris later that evening. If she left now, she could just make it. She could take matters into her own hands and show Tristan Falco exactly who she was.

'There will be no damage,' she said carefully, putting the last of her things into her gym bag before turning back. 'Not if Tristan Falco is as good a businessman as he claims to be. Now if you'll excuse me, I have a flight to catch.'

By the time Nina's limousine pulled up in front of Paris's stunning Musée des Arts Décoratifs, the sky over the city had faded to a pleasant brushwork of purples, pinks and oranges. The one benefit she enjoyed from the four years she'd spent at an elite all-girls boarding school in the Swiss Alps was the network of powerful women she now had dotted all across the globe. One of whom was Hermione Hall, a fashion stylist who had served to get her access to this particular event. Considering the ticket she'd nabbed was for a model who'd fallen sick at the last minute, she'd also been required to sport an haute couture gown for the evening.

Nina took one last look in her compact mirror at the finished result of the past hour of lightning-fast make-up and dress alterations. Fashion-world people truly were magicians—there was no other explanation for how they had managed to transform her from a tired, unpolished mess to whatever illusion of glamour this was. Her gown was a kind of powder-blue lace and tulle creation that clung to her body like a second skin from neck to mid-thigh, before flowing out into a long train behind her. A white glittering mask covered her from above her eyebrows to below her nose with glittering diamond appliqué making her sparkle as she moved in the light.

To most people, one couldn't get much luckier than getting the opportunity to dress up and play the part of a supermodel for one night. But she was a naturally intro-verted person with a rather complicated history with the press, and stepping out onto the red carpet outside the museum was quite frankly Nina's idea of hell on earth.

A wall of photographers and journalists seemed to command the throng of glamorous A-list carpet walkers in a shocking wave of sound that temporarily held her frozen still with its urgency. Anonymity wasn't neces-sary for her plan tonight to work, but she couldn't deny it was a lot easier to hold her head high without the weight of her family's world-famous downfall hanging over her.

The hum of voices tumbled over one another as she took a few shaky steps forward, feeling the comfort-ing glare of the event's security guards ensuring no-body got too close. The theme of the Falco Diamonds showcase was a summer masquerade and, once she'd made it halfway down the carpet without slipping, she focused on locating the only person she actually cared about seeing tonight. She was so distracted by the long line of famous faces that she almost missed him entirely.

'Tristan, over here!' a photographer called out, soon

joined by an echo of others, all scrambling for the perfect shot of the man of the hour.

Nina's breath caught as a man passed close by her, his sleeve just slightly brushing the skirt of her dress as he stepped out into the glare of the camera flashes. In a sea of black, his tuxedo was a brilliant white that seemed to make his dark blond hair and tanned skin glow. He wore no mask on his face. He stood a full foot taller than everyone around him, his blue eyes smouldering at the cameras as if he were some kind of fallen angel, sent to earth make every other human feel inferior. He owned every inch of the red carpet as a quartet of beautiful women posed and clung to his impressively muscular arms.

Who on earth needed to bring four dates to an event? She felt a flash of irritation as the women smiled and simpered up at him, while he all but ignored their presence. She knew that Falco carefully curated his wild playboy image and possibly was not actually involved with all four of the women. But the way their hands roamed over his torso as they moved as one spoke of a certain intimacy.

Was that even possible?

She was staring openly now, wondering at the...*practicality* of one man entertaining four women at once. Then again, if the rumours about Tristan Falco's insatiable appetite for bedroom gymnastics were true, perhaps this was the minimum number of participants required to maintain his attention. It had been all over social media when his girlfriend had left him a few months ago for his cousin—maybe one woman wasn't enough for Tristan Falco. Her inexperienced mind and overactive imagination attempted to conjure up an image and she couldn't help it, she laughed out loud with surprise at the absurdity of it.

There was no way her laugh could have been heard over the din of the crowds around them and yet she felt a prickle of awareness skate along her skin before she looked back up to see that she had become the sole focus of one man's attention.

She felt frozen in place as Falco's gaze blatantly dipped to languorously take in her figure before rising back up to meet her eyes with exaggerated slowness. The slow smile that transformed his lips was pure sin, his midnight-blue eyes sparking with the kind of devilish glint that she would have to be completely naïve not to understand.

'Miss Roux?'

She felt as if she were breaking out of a trance as she blinked, turning to find one of Hermione Hall's assistants standing by her side looking impatient.

'You need to get inside or all of the best pieces of jewellery to accompany this gown will be gone.' The woman urged her ahead and Nina dutifully followed, ignoring the strange prickle on the back of her neck as she moved inside the entryway.

For a man renowned for his wild playboy lifestyle and love of excess, Tristan Falco was never anything but fully in control at all times.

But tonight, he was distracted.

He usually adored playing host, a role that he had

been raised in as the only son of a world-famous Argentinian diamond heiress and global fashion icon. His mother had taught him how to work a crowd and how to use his charm and good looks to build a fortune of his own. He had long been a success in his own right, with his carefully curated image paving the way for his skills in the business world to slide under the radar just as he liked it. But that success had come with a certain level of disconnect.

He had long grown used to suffering through the company at A-list events, with people clamouring for his attention while he worked through his mental list of business connections and takeover bids. And of course, lately, with dodging the more and more overt attempts his mother was making at finding him a wife. Recent scandals in the press regarding his love life had done him no favours, but ever since her retirement as CEO of her beloved company, Dulce Falco had decided the time had come for her only son to settle down and give her grandchildren. Not even planning her own upcoming wedding in Buenos Aires had distracted her.

He loved his mother and didn't want to worry her… and having a wife and family of his own was an idea he had actually gradually been warming up to in recent times, not that he'd admit it. Until his ex had run off with his cousin and the ensuing scandal had served as a reminder that men like him were not built for domesticity.

Grabbing a second glass of champagne from a passing waiter, he tried to focus on his task list for the evening. He felt…on edge and it had nothing to do with the pressure he was under to marry and everything to do with finding out the identity of the mysterious beauty he'd seen outside.

Time and time again he had found his eyes searching for the woman in blue in the crowd, catching glimpses of her progress in between interruptions from his own less than captivating companions. She had been allocated a tiara from the exhibit to match the gown she wore; he knew the one from the antique jewellery collection being exhibited tonight by Falco Diamonds. He wore the matching crown on top of his own head, chosen weeks ago by his personal styling team.

As he downed the remnants of his glass of champagne and gestured for a refill, his eyes roamed the cavernous museum hall once more, taking only a few moments before finding the object of his thoughts.

She stood under one of the domes at the centre of the nave, her white mask glittering under the light show that had begun on the ceiling and upper walls. Utterly still, she gazed up at the cascade of blooms and stars that pulsated and blossomed above them. Around her, countless A-list attendees schmoozed and networked, but her gaze remained focused upon the lights above as though she were in a trance.

Or perhaps, just like him, she wished to be anywhere else but here.

It was easy to imagine slipping over there and introducing himself with his usual charm. He would tell her the story behind the inspiration between their headpieces, his own based on a coronet worn by the King of old Sardegna and hers the beautiful princess who became his queen. He would compliment her dress as he gazed into her eyes; they had seemed dark and soulful from what he could make out under the mask she wore. From there, the game of seduction would begin and it would be only a matter of time before he was peeling her out of that blue lace and she was crying out his name.

He cleared his suddenly dry throat, shocked at how quickly his thoughts had descended into depravity. His libido had barely stirred all evening as his four beautiful dates had made a show of flirting and touching him at every opportunity. He hadn't bedded a woman in months, hadn't felt genuine interest in even longer. As if to prove his point, his last remaining neglected date finally reached her limit and sighed loudly before stalking away in search of more attentive entertainment. The distraction caused him to lose track of the blue-lace beauty once more and he cursed under his breath.

'Tristan, why am I not surprised that you chose a crown?'

His entire body stiffening at the familiar feminine voice, he turned to find scarlet-tipped nails clawed upon his white tuxedo sleeve. His ex-lover Gabriela, owner of said claws, leaned in for the customary Argentinian greeting of one single kiss upon his right cheek. Before he had a moment to prepare, he was engulfed in her cloying scent. A scent that had once seemed seductive and warm, but now served only as a reminder that the prettiest flowers were quite often the ones that held the most venom.

'You managed to snag an invite.' He smiled, steeling his jaw against any hint of the anger that seeing her here at his event provoked in him. 'What a surprise.'

'Surprise? Don't tell me Vic hasn't spoken to you yet?' She sighed, turning just as they were joined by another person he would rather claw his own eyes out than speak to tonight. His cousin.

'He's impossible to track down.' Victor Falco laughed, the humour not quite meeting his eyes as he looked anxiously between Gabriela and the man they'd both publicly humiliated just a few short months before. 'I was wondering who had selected the King's crown piece. I should have known it was you.'

'I thought the sapphires would bring out my big, beautiful eyes,' Tristan gritted.

'Bring out your massive ego more like,' Victor teased, but the once easy joking between them was no more, and so the barb only rubbed.

Tristan resisted the urge to growl, taking a sip of champagne. 'How could anyone have an ego with you two always nearby, primed to kick them back to earth?'

Victor opened his mouth as if to retaliate, only for the tension to be broken by the return of one of Tristan's dates, who insisted upon hand-feeding him a chocolate-covered strawberry. A second date appeared toting a fresh flute of champagne, both women leaning in to drape themselves across his arms.

'Good to see you're not too heartbroken, anyway.' Gabriela let out a delicate sniff of disbelief.

'Amazing what inheriting control over a multibillion-dollar corporation will do for one's sex appeal.'

'Charming as always, Tristan.' Victor frowned repressively. 'I had thought recent events might have made you more serious.'

'Which events are you referring to, *primo*?' Tristan said darkly, his body tensing at the disapproving tone of his cousin's voice. 'The fact that my mother chose *me* as her replacement on the board...or the fact that I had to take that seat under a cloud of scandal caused by you?'

The air between them seemed to crackle with a sudden intensity. Victor was only a couple of months older than him, hardly the voice of wisdom. They had been more than family. Tristan had once counted him his closest friend. But at some point in the past year, Victor had grown increasingly distant towards him. And a large part of the reason for that distance currently stood between them with a shiny diamond ring on her finger and her hand delicately cradling her stomach. Her very obviously *rounded* stomach.

'I see congratulations are in order,' he said, pasting on a serene smile even as his gut roiled.

'I thought Victor had already told you.' Gabriela breathed the incredulous words, which seemed surprisingly genuine, while Victor simply gritted his jaw and brooded.

'How could I have told him when he avoids me at all costs?'

'Well, now I know.' Tristan shrugged, downing the remainder of his champagne. 'I see a large diamond ring as well, so it seems my cousin was an easier man to pressure than me. Bravo.'

Gabriela inhaled a sharp breath, painted lips parting in a mixture of shock and anger. Tristan felt another uncomfortable twist in his gut as he watched Victor lean down to his fiancée, touching a hand possessively to his unborn child as he whispered something into her ear. With a final sharp look in his direction, she turned and walked away. Disappointingly, Victor did not follow.

'This is neither the time nor the place for our personal issues.' Victor muttered angrily. 'This exhibit honours our family's legacy and you show up in typical playboy style with an orgy of partners.'

'I will not apologise for the fact that I am in high demand,' Tristan felt his mouth tighten with a cruel smile. 'Since you so selfishly took yourself off the market, my workload has doubled.'

His cousin shook his head, eyes narrowing. 'Your mother told me what you promised her, along with taking the helm.'

'That's my business.'

'So it's true?' Victor's brows rose. 'You're finally going to settle down with a wife and family?'

'I'm going to give my mother the grand wedding she craves, with the perfect bride.' Tristan tugged at his collar, feeling it tighten around his neck like a noose. He inhaled and pasted on his most rake-like smirk. 'I never promised anything about settling down.'

'You've already found the lucky lady in question?'

'You seem very interested in my love life, cousin; have you already tired of the last fiancée you stole from me?'

There was no trace of mirth in Victor's eyes as he stepped forward, closing the small space between them. 'You weren't engaged. I've tried to explain countless times. Gabi and I never set out to hurt you.'

For a brief moment, he imagined the satisfaction he

would get from punching his cousin squarely in the jaw. But ultimately he decided that the sight of Victor clutching at his own broken nose, while highly deserved and overdue, would not be worth the ruination of his pristine white tux.

'As I've said, I'm over it,' Tristan snapped, pulling his arm away. 'Now, if you'll excuse me, I have a fiancée to track down.'

He walked away, leaving his cousin stuttering with outrage while he moved along the lavish gallery under the pretence of greeting the other guests, but, really, he was hunting. His skin vibrated with awareness as he scanned the crowd gathered around the cases of priceless jewels, his steps slow and measured. A shimmering cloud of blue caught his attention like a moonbeam in the darkness and he looked up, catching sight of her in the reflection of the glass case in front of him. He looked over his shoulder, just in time to see her slide sideways behind a mannequin.

Interesting.

Testing his theory, he moved along the crowd to another case, and sure enough a shimmer of blue followed a few moments later, partially obscured by a large wall of diamond-encrusted flowers. Curiosity burning now, he continued to amble slowly along the crowded floor, calmly waving off the calls of attention from various business contacts. A few moments were all he would need to ascertain who she was and assuage this fixation. Then he could return to the event clear-minded and hopefully with a plan in place for his mystery lady later tonight.

His pulse quickening, he made sure she still tailed him as he made a series of turns until he reached an empty hallway. There, he slipped through a balcony door...and waited.

CHAPTER TWO

SHE HAD LOST HIM.

Nina looked from one edge of the darkened terrace to the other, squinting in the low light. She'd spent the past hour discreetly tailing Tristan Falco from afar, waiting for an opportunity to sidetrack him and make her move. For someone who had avoided the paddock as a new owner under the guise of being far too busy, the infuriating man had a remarkable flare for striking up a conversation with every passer-by with a pulse. Not only that, it was very clear that he was hosting the entire event.

Her irritation had grown as she'd watched him glide effortlessly between the influential guests that filled the long gallery, a grand crown atop his head as if he owned the entire museum. Which he did not. She had already done a quick search on her phone to check. The Falco family were probably the biggest benefactors, with their historic jewellery and gem collection being one of the grandest exhibits in Europe.

She had already been exhausted after the weekend of racing events, followed by *that* press conference and the subsequent mad dash to get here, and she was now feeling the effects. Her insides felt too tight, her thoughts moving too fast. Events like this served only to remind her of her childhood in Monte Carlo, back when the Roux name had been a golden ticket to every elite event in the city. Her mother had wanted to parade her only daughter around in all the latest fashions like a doll, then grown furious when Nina had struggled to behave correctly. She'd been told she was too sensitive. Too different. *Too much.*

But, for Nina, the high-society world had been what felt like too much. The scratchy clothing, the dancing, the unwritten rules, the constant noise and banal chat. The only way she'd managed to cope was by zoning out to the happy place in her mind, imagining she was navigating the trickiest chicane in the Circuit de Monaco or flying along the final straight to victory at the Autodromo Accardi.

On the track she wasn't too sensitive or weird or wrong. Her attention to detail and her immovable focus were what made her a damn great driver. The only time she'd ever felt *right* was behind the wheel of a racing car with her aunt Lola's words ringing in her mind, to ask herself not *if* she could become a world champion but *when*. She refused to lose that determination and let a bunch of clueless men in suits break her down. She wouldn't let them win.

A balmy breeze blew across her flushed cheeks and she prayed she wouldn't cry. She ached to remove the false lashes on her lids, feeling rather like a prisoner in a cage of modern beauty standards. The haute couture gown was too heavy and felt like sandpaper on her skin.

Bracing her hands on the stone balustrade, she drew a hearty breath and growled with frustration, letting go of some of her tightly held restraint in the solitude of the dark terrace, adding a string of curses under her breath for good measure.

'Looking for someone?'

Nina jumped, peering over her shoulder to find a man looming in a shadowy alcove beside the doorway she'd just exited through. A loud squeak escaped her lips as her body seemed to react of its own accord, her hands slipping on the balcony ledge, sending her sliding sideways until her hip bone thumped painfully into the cold stone.

When she looked up, the man had moved out of the shadows, a familiar sapphire-encrusted crown glinting atop his head and white tuxedo jacket glowing in the moonlight.

Falco.

Her eyes narrowed upon the man she'd been seeking for much longer than one night, the man who had hijacked all of her plans and taken her dreams, stamping them under his shiny billionaire shoes. He stared at her, eyes hooded and the hint of a smirk dancing upon his full lips. He really was sinfully handsome, for a spineless jerk.

'Why yes, as a matter of fact.' She stepped forward. 'I'm here to—'

'Take off your mask,' he interjected silkily.

Nina inhaled sharply. 'Excuse me? That's not exactly—'

'Take off your mask...*por favor.*'

'Do you always bark commands at strangers in the dark by way of greeting?' she snapped.

'Only if said stranger has unashamedly stalked me from the moment she arrived at this event.'

She felt her cheeks heat, another flare of irritation at herself for how utterly terribly this plan was going.

'Did you hope for me not to notice your eyes on me, *belleza*?' He took another step forward. 'Or is this all part of your game for me this evening? Because I'll admit I'm hoping for the latter.'

Belleza? Her game? What kind of riddles was this man talking in? She opened her mouth to speak, only to feel a warm fingertip press ever so slightly against her lips. Eyes wide, she fought the urge to bite it off.

'There is no need to be embarrassed,' he continued, oblivious to the danger his digit was in. 'I admire a woman who sees what she wants and tracks it down unapologetically. I noticed you from the moment that you stepped onto the carpet outside. I found myself… irrevocably intrigued. I know everyone here. But you are a mystery.'

'Everyone here is wearing a mask,' she pointed out. 'Everyone except you, Your Highness.'

His smile widened at the sarcastic honorific, his ego clearly enjoying a thorough stroke. Her mind's eye immediately conjured an image of herself smacking that smile from his pompous, arrogant, perfectly sculpted lips. She paused at that last descriptor, wondering why looking at those lips made her feel too warm all of a sudden. He noticed where her gaze had wandered and his smirk turned utterly sinful.

'Take off the mask,' he murmured again. 'Or are you waiting for me to remove it for you?'

'I dare you to try.' She spoke through gritted teeth.

'Do you realise your eyes practically glowed just now?' he mused, pursing his lips as he trailed a fingertip along the edge of her mask. 'Quite an achievement, considering they are such a deep brown that they're practically black. Like tourmaline…or the rarest obsidian.'

The sudden bubble of laughter that escaped Nina's throat took her by surprise, but once she released it she could no longer hold back.

'Something amusing?' he asked, his charming mask slipping ever so slightly.

'It's just…the pretty Spanish endearments, describing eyeballs like rare gems et cetera. Do you speak to every woman you meet with such flowery words?'

'Are you trying to puncture my ego on purpose?' He feigned injury, pressing a tanned hand to his chest. 'Or is this how you flirt?'

'I think you know that I'm not here for vacuous flirtation.'

'No, I can tell that you're different. You're here with a purpose, aren't you?' he said softly. 'How lucky that we find ourselves having a rare and magical moment on this deserted terrace.'

'Of course.' She let out another tinny breath of laughter. 'I'm different. I'm *special*.'

'You are…certainly fascinating,' he countered. 'And not at all what I expected to find when I lured you out here.'

'I was not *lured*, I followed you.' She paused, a blush

climbing her cheeks at the immediate expression of victory on his smug face. Damn him. Fully tired of this *game*, as he'd called it, she swept the white mask from her face and waited for his immediate recognition and apology. None came.

His eyes roamed her face, the tense silence that followed making her feel as if she were under a microscope. When he finally spoke, his voice held an odd rasp, as though it vibrated directly out from the depths of his chest.

'*There* you are, *belleza*.'

There was something familiar about her. Something he couldn't quite put his finger on. As though they had met before, but he knew all too well that if they had, he would have remembered her. He was not a man prone to fascination. He had become jaded with the frequency of intimate situations such as this, of people practically throwing themselves in his path once they had heard the rumours of his sensual prowess. Rumours that had begun during a particularly intense time in his life and had never quite left him.

Of course, many of the things that had been said about him were completely true. But that was beside the point.

Perhaps that was why this delectable woman was making him feel as if his chest were suddenly too tight beneath his skin. She was young and beautiful and yet she seemed entirely unimpressed by him, almost irritated by his silky words and practised compliments. It was refreshing... And did absolutely nothing to calm the raging heat that had been steadily building within him from the moment he'd seen her delicate features up close.

Without the mask, the full perfection of her face had assaulted him, those focused obsidian eyes perfectly framed by dark brows and delicately rounded cheeks. Her lips were lush and full, certainly kissable, but it was the small dimple in her chin that caught his attention most. A stubborn chin, currently tilted up at him as if to emphasise that very fact.

She hadn't made any move to push him away, or go back inside, so he knew that her protestations were likely a part of her gambit. Perhaps she had heard the rumours that he was seeking a wife and was fearlessly offering herself up for the cause.

He would reward her bravery, quite thoroughly if given the chance. Images of peeling her out of that sparkling blue confection sprang to his mind, not doing anything to help the rather *pressing* situation threatening below his belt.

'Nothing to say?' she asked, a strangely expectant expression on her pixie-like face. The make-up she wore was pronounced, too pronounced for his liking. He had the sudden urge to see her freshly washed, scrubbed free of any excess. In his shower preferably after a night of vigorous lovemaking.

'I would offer up more compliments, but you've made it clear you have no need for them. Instead, let's talk about why you're here,' he said simply.

'I would think it's quite obvious why I'm here,' she

answered softly. 'You're a notoriously difficult man to pin down.'

'And you believe that you are the woman for the job?'

'I wouldn't have come all this way if I didn't. Of course, I'm quite busy and would have preferred for you to come to me...for us to have discussed this in a more appropriate setting. But this will have to do.'

Tristan smiled, surprised at how very much he was enjoying her directness. For a man in urgent need of a fiancée to put his mother's matchmaking to rest, he couldn't do much better than this woman if he'd tried. He wouldn't do something so foolish as to actually *marry* her, of course. But he could enjoy exploring this hypothetical negotiation of theirs for a little longer.

'A more formal setting?' he asked silkily. 'The nearest courthouse perhaps?'

'There's no need to rush straight to legalities. I heard you were a more skilled negotiator than that?' She looked away, a small frown appearing between her brows. 'I'm not interested in a public spectacle. I followed you here tonight to discuss the benefits for us both in getting this done quickly.'

Again, words left him for a moment. He simply stared, utterly baffled at the rush of exhilaration coursing through him. She was speaking of marriage, for goodness' sake. He should be running a mile. Just what kind of spell had she put over him?

'Are you expecting a proposal right here on this terrace?'

She frowned at his words. 'At the very least I'm expecting an attempt at negotiation. A display of your notorious skills before you allow me to walk away. Because, trust me, I am fully prepared to do that.'

'You would deny yourself the experience of my... *skills* so easily?' He stepped forward, close enough that the skirt of her dress pooled against his knees. 'Are you not curious to see me in action?'

Her eyes widened, her neck lengthening prettily as she looked up at him through hooded lashes. Ah yes, the guile of innocence... Not one of his favourite performances but one that he could appreciate, nonetheless. Here she was waylaying him with the hopes of dazzling him into a proposal and when all else failed she would play the naïve damsel, completely unaware of her sensual prowess.

'I'm sure you're quite impressive,' she said breathlessly, her eyes still trained on his lips. 'I don't want to walk away, allow me to be perfectly clear on that point. But I know that you'd be a fool to let me go. I know how valuable I am.'

'Like a rare gem, in fact?'

Her nostrils flared, one pointed finger rising to poke him in the chest. 'Don't mock me, Falco. I'm not here to play.'

He grabbed her hand, holding it captive against the spot where his heart beat frantically against his ribcage. Those obsidian eyes glowed up at him once again with irritation and he was done for. He'd give her whatever she wanted just to see that passion in another, more intimate setting.

'*Playing* is the best way to negotiate, *cariña*.' He laid a single tentative kiss against the inside of the wrist he held captive. 'It's my favourite way, in fact. But we will need to take this meeting somewhere more private if I hope to give you my full attention.'

'Somewhere private,' she repeated slowly, her eyes glued to the point where his lips still pressed against her skin. 'Okay...'

'I can have my driver meet us out front in five minutes,' he murmured, urgency rapidly taking control of his libido as he slowly drew her closer. 'And I can have you naked and calling out my name in ten.'

She looked up at him, and he caught a brief view of her eyes widening in surprise before he lowered his lips to hers. The heat of her mouth against his was like a fire in his blood and he suddenly doubted if they would make it to the car at all. It felt like a lifetime since he'd experienced this kind of unbridled desire for a woman.

He paused, realising she hadn't moved since he'd kissed her—in fact, she was as still as a statue. He moved to pull back, only to hear the smallest moan escape her lips. Her hands slid up to wrap around his neck and suddenly she was kissing him back frantically, albeit with very little control or finesse.

A roar of victory coursed through his veins and he scooped her up, pressing her back against the stone balustrade and tilting his head to gain deeper access. He needed to taste every inch of her and have her do the same to him. He needed her wild for him. As though she heard his thoughts, her tongue delved into his mouth in a perfect imitation of his own, giving just as good as she got. Just as he'd thought, she was a little firebrand. *Dios*, but he was half tempted to take her right here on the balcony, no questions asked. He didn't even know her name.

Perhaps he'd keep it that way, keep the air of mystery between them for tonight, then once they'd both been thoroughly satisfied he'd deal with the aftermath. The real world could wait. Everything could wait.

Vaguely, he was aware of a sudden flash of white light. His mystery woman froze in his arms and for a moment he wondered if lightning had struck. How very poetic that would be. But as a second burst of light surrounded them, his sex-addled mind finally processed that it was the unmistakable flash of a camera bulb. Rearing back, he turned just as a third flash bathed the terrace with white light and briefly illuminated a young woman holding up a phone on the next terrace.

'Mierda,' he growled, gently lowering his equally kiss-addled companion down to her feet before moving quickly towards the iron railing that separated the two balconies. The woman with the phone had already begun running in the opposite direction, but if they moved quickly his security team might catch up to her. He had to, if he wanted any chance of stopping those photos from getting out. His promise to his mother ringing in his ears, he made the call and felt his chest release slightly when he was assured that his team were on the case. It would be fine, everything would be fine and he would still be free to continue exploring his little interlude with the woman in blue.

That particular thought renewing his lust, he spun around to find the terrace was now empty and all trace of his mystery woman gone.

CHAPTER THREE

NINA UPPED HER maximum speed on the treadmill, pushing herself into a sprint. She was all alone in the Falco Roux private fitness facility, with most of the team taking a rest day. With the idea of rest being utterly laughable, she'd chosen to complete a punishing session of strength and mobility work. She pushed herself past her usual limits, making the excuse that she needed to get some heavy cardio in after a long night travelling back to Monaco from Paris. In truth, she was simply trying to take a break from the constant notifications on her phone and the threat of Astrid Lewis appearing like an anxious PR damage-control fairy behind her at any moment.

She had messed up, royally.

The photos of her and Tristan Falco kissing had appeared on a gossip site late last night and had spread like wildfire across social media within hours. Even with all the money that Tristan Falco had, no one could stop the power of the Internet. They were the top trending topic on most social media sites and if he hadn't known who she was last night, he certainly did now with headlines like *The Roux-mours Are True* and *Falco's Driving Her*

Crazy titillating the masses. She'd stopped looking after the first few, utterly unable to stare at another image of her one moment of weakness.

She wasn't even quite sure how it had happened. She wasn't the best judge of context most of the time, but add in the kind of intense charm that Tristan Falco exuded and, quite simply, her mental processing had been compromised. He'd mistaken her for someone else, that much was for sure with the kind of things he'd been saying. But who he might have mistaken her for was an utter mystery. She had gone over and over their conversation in her mind, trying to pick at which point things had begun to unravel past her control.

Her mind conjured up an HD slow-motion reel of the moment his lips had touched the inside of her wrist and she was shocked at the immediate flush of warmth that swirled behind her bellybutton.

Yeah, that had been the start of it, all right.

One thing was for sure, the rumours about ultimate playboy Tristan Falco were not at all false. And apparently, she had come perilously close to experiencing his skills first-hand. Even the small taste she had received had felt like being hooked up to a live electricity source. He was brutally intense, and she had never reacted to anyone physically like that. Not a single person.

It was why she'd never felt any urge to go on dates, or pursue flirtations with the many guys who'd expressed intense curiosity about thawing the so-called Elite One Ice Princess. It wasn't an act or a measure of self-preservation; she simply wasn't interested. She was always in control and she never forgot who she was and what she wanted.

Well, almost never.

Punching the speed even higher, she ran and ran until she thought she might come close to pulling a muscle and then she stopped and cooled down, staring out at the view of the harbour for a long time before forcing herself to go and shower. She lingered longer than usual under the hot spray, once again feeling lucky that she was the only female driver on the team and had an entire bathroom to herself. She'd managed to avoid the rest of the team since arriving at their relatively deserted headquarters, but she was no fool, she knew that she couldn't avoid them for ever. Any respect she'd had as a driver was now compromised, with her name being dragged through the mud.

The idea that she'd been seen *kissing* their new playboy owner… Scandal like that was bound to cause trouble. Would all of the work she'd done to be seen as an equal to the male drivers be reset and disregarded? Reputations were everything in this high-drama sport and she had just painted a target on her back. She'd already been branded as a pay driver, a term given to minimise the talent of drivers who were related to their team owner. But she'd proven herself time and time again as she'd risen up through the ranks, showing her skill while still acknowledging the enormous privilege she'd experienced as a member of the Roux family.

There was no fancy term she knew of for a driver who was perceived to be sleeping with the team owner, but she was pretty sure the public would come up with plenty. None of which would be remotely complimentary to her.

With a single kiss, Tristan Falco had possibly landed the final nail in the coffin of her short-lived career. Or perhaps she had done that herself by allowing her temper to take hold and travelling to Paris to confront him incognito. He hadn't forced himself on her after all. She could have stopped him at any moment. Much as she'd like to pretend that she hadn't been in full possession of her senses, in fact the opposite was true. A handsome man had shown her the slightest bit of attention and she'd melted into his embrace like butter. She'd been painfully aware of every touch, every look, every slide of his lips against hers.

She was twenty-three and hadn't experienced a true kiss of passion until last night. She wasn't embarrassed about that fact—her lack of experience wasn't something she thought about often at all. It was easy not to think about sex when you didn't particularly feel or engage in sexual attraction. But with Falco, she'd felt far too much. Now she wondered, if they hadn't been interrupted, would she have stopped him at all?

Her nipples pebbled painfully and she blamed the air conditioning, shaking off her thoughts as she stepped out of the shower. Her reflection in the mirror was a cruel reminder of the real reason Falco hadn't recognised her when she'd removed her mask last night. Her black hair hung limply to her shoulders, not quite curly but not quite straight either. Dark circles underlined her red-rimmed eyes, framed by a face most in the media had delighted in describing as plain and uninteresting.

Most people outside the media described her that way too. They seemed to make a point to comment on her supposed lack of femininity, analysing her ungraceful gait and her far too casual dress sense. Traits that the men in her industry generally did not have to accentuate or play up to. She'd long ago stopped bothering to challenge their boring ideals.

Still, she couldn't help but wonder would the playboy find her so *fascinating* if he could see her now? She pushed the thought away, reminding herself that Falco's opinion of her did not matter. What mattered most right now was to try and figure out a way to see if anything in this workplace nightmare was salvageable. Perhaps she could use this to get her contract fully cancelled, maybe get in ahead of the news to one of the other teams, offer to sign a scandalously low contract with them… Even as the thought crossed her mind she pushed it away, knowing that the legal ramifications would bankrupt her if she tried to do that.

'You *are* fascinating,' she told her reflection in the mirror. 'Fascinatingly gifted at tanking your own career.'

A knock on the door startled her out of her thoughts and she rushed to wrap a towel around herself before answering, betting it was Sophie come to chastise her for working too hard. It took her a moment of stunned blinking to realise that the handsome blond besuited man standing on the other side was not her trainer, but Tristan Falco. With a squeak, she threw the door closed again.

'I've already seen you, so there's no point in hiding. We need to talk.'

She held her breath, pressing herself back against

the cool tiled wall and fighting the urge to groan at her own terrible life choices. Realistically, how long could she hide in here before he gave up? Her gym bag with all of her things was on the other side of the door and he knew she was in here. She wasn't the only one who'd been dealing with a personal PR nightmare for the past twelve hours. He hadn't come all this way for a casual chat.

As if to prove that point, he rapped on the door once again. 'Nina. We don't have time for this. I'm here to discuss urgent matters.'

Her name in his silky voice sent a shiver down her spine—of trepidation, she was sure. This man was her team owner, her boss's boss. The person who controlled every cent that kept the racing team she loved alive. Like it or not, she had to at least try to plead her case to him. She had to fight.

'Do you plan to hide in there all day?' His voice was a rough rasp on the other side of the door, his impatience clear. 'Your little photo stunt in Paris has created a situation that requires immediate action.'

Irritation won out over modesty and before she knew it, Nina was flinging open the door to face him once more. '*My* little stunt?' she fumed. 'I'm not the one who was comparing my eyes to diamonds and bragging about my *skills*.'

His eyes briefly lowered to take in her towel-clad form before his jaw set and he met her gaze head-on. 'I didn't know who you were.'

'That says more about you than me, considering you've owned my family's racing team for more than a year.' She ignored the wave of embarrassment threatening to drown her and focused on her anger and indignation. 'I never court the press and I had nothing to do with that photo. I followed you because you are impossible to meet with and I needed to convince you to cancel my contract. That's the only reason I went to Paris.'

Falco's eyes narrowed, a hand absent-mindedly rising to scrub along the shadow of stubble along his jawline. 'Did you kiss me in the hope I would fire you?'

'No.' Nina gasped, her cheeks heating. 'And you kissed *me.*'

His eyes darkened. 'It's irrelevant who initiated it… because your contract is not up for negotiation. Surely you know that. You're the only remaining family member working in a team that thrives on superstition. A team that I've been trying to rescue and bring back to glory, but been met with public resistance at every turn. I may not be a racing expert, but I've done my research. The only thing that has *not* been against us is having you locked into a five-year term.'

Nina closed her eyes, knowing that he was right. Knowing that the superstition the Roux fans held was ridiculous, but that didn't make it any less real. It had been the only reason that had kept her here over the past couple of years since her brother had brought their family's finances to the brink of collapse. They had only ever been without a Roux on the team for a handful of seasons, and each one of those had been plagued with crashes and incidents bringing them nothing but ruin.

'Perhaps you should have thought of that before you signed Apollo Accardi instead of promoting your hardest-working and best-performing reserve driver.' Nina stood up tall, wishing she'd at least been wearing her gym shorts for this altercation. But she was here now, so she might as well say her piece.

He tilted his head to the side, surveying her with keen interest. 'You expected the promotion to fall to you instead of a former world champion with years of track experience?'

'I expected at the very least an attempt at showing me some respect, some form of communication to explain why the usual protocol was being changed to make way for a completely new driver mid-season instead of the obvious replacement, yes.' Nina stood her ground, ignoring the flash of awareness in her gut that she felt with his eyes on her. 'But it really shouldn't have surprised me, considering the way you do business.'

Tristan tried to ignore the way Nina's cheeks flushed as her temper rose. The woman was furious with him, that much was abundantly clear. Suddenly her aloof attitude from the night before made infinitely more sense. She'd been in a mask and haute couture, but as he'd surmised—scrubbed clean, she was still strikingly beautiful.

Pulling his attention back to the conversation at hand, he tried to resolve his unusually scattered thoughts. He'd come here to ascertain if her appearance last night had been with the intent to sabotage the team, or deliberately cause a scandal. Now that he was relatively sure it had been a misunderstanding on both of their parts, he had an even more difficult job to do—convince her to help him.

'Exactly how do I do business, Miss Roux?' He purred, 'Please, enlighten me.'

'You buy up failing companies and sell them off, with very little close contact or sentiment,' she responded easily. 'That tactic might work in a hedge fund or a faceless corporation, but it won't work here. You may have put your name up front, but Roux Racing was built on passion and loyalty.'

Passion. Loyalty. The way she said the words with such conviction, it was clear she truly believed them. Perhaps in this case, she was right. 'My ownership style is not why you weren't consulted on the Accardi deal. We secured the signing of the decade that will give us a psychological and strategic edge against our biggest competitor. Surprise was essential.'

She didn't answer him immediately, instead she grabbed her gym bag and disappeared momentarily into a screened-off area, no doubt to change into some clothing. He took the chance to steer the conversation to his ultimate goal. To the reason why he'd chosen to race here himself today, instead of sending his PR team in his place to clean up the mess. Tristan Falco never missed an opportunity to capitalise on a business opportunity, and Nina might not know it yet, but their kiss had unwittingly become the answer to both of their problems.

'Speaking of passion, Astrid has informed me that the photo of us kissing has officially gone viral.' He waited a moment, taking a seat on the long bench that lined the wall of the dressing room.

She reappeared from behind the screen in a pair of

white gym shorts and a loose-fitting Falco Roux polo shirt. 'You say that like it's a positive thing.'

'Actually, my team seems to think it's the answer to all of our PR issues.'

Nina immediately stiffened and shook her head, jet-black waves shaking gently with the movement. 'For you, perhaps. I'm sure the comments about me aren't quite the same.'

He slid his phone out of his pocket, pulling up the curated list of comments that Astrid had forwarded him an hour before. They included gushing viral clips from critics and romantics and superstitious old-timer racing buffs alike. The list also included an unheard-of increase in the sale of Falco Roux merchandise, stock and race tickets over the past twelve hours, which was predicted only to grow as the news continued to spread. He watched as Nina read through the data, her keen eyes rising back to his with stunned understanding.

'These comments…they're all positive. Happy, even.'

'Apparently the fans love us together. And the stockholders love it when the fans are happy. This is great for the team.'

She crossed her arms. 'So this is why you came here. To ask me to go along with a lie for publicity?'

Tristan crossed his arms. 'I expected a true business mind would see this as the golden bargaining opportunity that it is.'

'You're suddenly open to negotiation?' She paused, one cynical brow quirking.

'My offer is simple. Stay. Play the paddock romance out until the end of the season and you're free to go.'

'Just like that?' She moved to the end of the bench, her hands twisting over and over in a strangely entrancing motion. When her eyes met his, they were stark. 'What if I say no?'

Tristan paused, measuring his words carefully before he spoke. 'If you try to leave for another team, then this goes exactly the same way it has gone for every other driver who has tried to break their contract. No special treatment.'

Nina closed her eyes. She knew what that meant. Legal battles, public defamation, and her reputation as a spoilt princess would become even more prominent. But there was still a chance she'd be bankrupt even if she saw the full contract out. Reserve drivers' wages didn't pay nearly enough to cover the her annual racing licence fees and other costs, not now that she was maintaining the cost of running the girls academy fully by herself. She'd have to downsize, maybe even close down for good and disappoint all of the talented young girls around the world who looked up to her and relied on her guidance.

Nina ran a hand through her hair. 'So my choice is to stay put for the next two years and waste more time as a reserve, or compromise my integrity by playing the part of the billionaire owner's girlfriend for the next few months. That's great, just great.'

'Fiancée,' Tristan said silkily, his eyes pinning her in place.

'What? Why?' Nina felt her words tumbling over her tongue but was powerless to stop them. Nothing about this interaction was anywhere close to being in her comfort zone and it just seemed to be getting worse with every new piece of information he divulged.

'My mother has recently been pressuring me to marry, and until last night I was in the market to fulfil that wish. If we go ahead with encouraging this PR fire for the next few months, it'll give me time without her breathing down my neck. I need it to benefit me as well.'

The mention of his *needs* made her breath catch and her traitorous imagination run wild with images of what such needs might entail. She pushed them away, trying to focus her business mind on the offer as a whole. Trying to make sure she wasn't being led astray.

'If I say yes, what would this deal entail?' she asked slowly, nibbling on the edge of a fingernail. 'Just holding hands in public every now and then?'

'Initially, we would just continue to stir speculation, capitalise on the current interest by being seen often together in the public eye.'

'And once that part is done?' she pressed.

'We would eventually announce our engagement and use our individual images to benefit one another: my presence at more of your races and your presence in my upcoming Falco Diamonds centenary campaign, that kind of thing. I will also require your attendance as my fiancée at my mother's wedding in Buenos Aires, but we'll be there for the Argentinian race, anyway. Don't worry; behind closed doors, this relationship will be purely platonic. It'll be safer for us both that way.'

'So it wouldn't be a big commitment, then. Time-wise, I mean?' she asked, mulling over the potential pitfalls and struggling to find any that weren't in favour of agreeing to this mad plan. 'With your decision to bring in a completely new driver mid-season, I won't have much spare time, Mr Falco.'

'You'll make time for me, *Nina*,' he said calmly, without missing a beat.

Nina ignored the thoroughly inappropriate pulse of awareness that thrummed through her at his words. 'With all due respect, *Tristan*, as a professional driver, I have a very demanding job.'

'Duly noted, but as my *fiancée* you will go where I go. Starting right now.' He eyed her Falco Roux polo shirt. 'You might want to change. I've made a lunch reservation at Blu Mont.'

'I haven't actually agreed to anything yet.' She looked down at her shorts and running shoes. 'And besides, I find it hard to see how anyone with a pair of eyes will believe that you're planning to marry *me* whether I'm in my uniform or a ballgown.'

He stepped closer. 'You'd better start convincing yourself, then. Because once you agree, this deal begins immediately.'

CHAPTER FOUR

IF HE'D THOUGHT the sight of Nina braless in her slightly translucent Falco Roux polo shirt had been a distraction, nothing could have prepared him for how she looked in a pair of jeans. She'd brushed her hair out so that it flowed around her face and donned a simple white T-shirt and red leather jacket. It was laughable that some of the media articles he'd read had referred to her as plain—considering his blood pressure hadn't quite stabilised since he'd walked in on her in nothing but a towel.

Some casual lunches and sightings of them together in public would be just enough to add more fuel to the fire before they officially confirmed their relationship to the press at a more strategic time. Astrid had been specific in her directions, and he trusted his PR manager implicitly, which was why he'd told her the truth. She was the best in the business, and if anyone could use this situation to their benefit, it was her.

He knew all too well that the key to selling a narrative was in the details, and so as he directed Nina to precede him onto the exclusive restaurant's very publicly visible seafront terrace he made sure to touch her elbow and guide her with his hand in the small of her back. Once she was seated, he trailed his fingers along the back of her chair, leaning down to lay a gentle caress upon her cheek before taking his own seat.

As he predicted, she was a little less relaxed about their ruse, those expressive eyes throwing daggers at him across the table every couple of moments as she intently focused upon her menu and not him.

'Have I done something to upset you, *mi cielo*?' he asked, reaching a hand out to cover hers with his own. She pulled away, hastily taking a long sip of water.

'The photographer isn't here yet,' she said quietly, returning her attention to the menu.

'This isn't just about appearing in more photos. Everyone who sees us should be under no illusion that we are an item.'

'These people are all looking at you, they barely even know who I am. Nor do they particularly care.'

'You're the daughter of one of the most famous families in Monaco.' He frowned, noting the way her hands anxiously twirled her napkin around her index finger.

'Infamous,' she corrected. 'We fell out of favour with the public long ago, as you well know.'

He knew a lot, of course. As part of acquiring a company in debt, it was his job to dig deep and know everything about what had got them there before he committed and planned his strategy. He knew about her great-grandfather's brilliance as an auto engineer and how he'd founded and ruled his empire with an iron fist, raising an army of his own children to carry on his legacy with their innovative designs and racing wins. Her own father had been a truly terrible businessman plagued with a catalogue of personal vices, and her aunt, Lola Roux, had been a racing legend in her own right before she'd died in a tragically ironic car accident.

Most recently, her reckless brother, Alain, had been happily draining the last of their funds for his lavish lifestyle, ending with him losing everything to Tristan in a high-stakes poker match. Said poker match was how Tristan had inadvertently ended up in his current position as the new team owner. What had happened, and the deal he'd made afterwards with Alain to try and save the Roux company, was not public knowledge and iron-clad non-disclosure agreements had been signed, but still he wondered just how much Nina knew, and if she potentially shared any of the vices of her more scandalous family members, other than the obvious thrill for speed.

'You believe your family's financial downfall has made you less interesting to the press?' he asked. 'That's not how it works.'

'My mother was the most in demand with the press, but, of course, they took an interest in me for a while once I was old enough and began attending parties.' Nina took another sip of water, pursing her lips into a thin line. 'They would take strategic shots of me at bad angles to make it look like I was some kind of party girl. Like mother, like daughter. But I didn't want to be a society princess. I preferred working, being on the track. Once I stopped attending any events or socialising outside work at all, they switched to the unlikable, plain Jane, ice-princess angle. Quite predictable really, yet I much prefer it.'

He surveyed the measured lack of interest on her

face, and the way she pressed her fingertips down flat into the tablecloth. She spoke of the press's interest in her calmly, but he had always been an expert in reading people. Everything about this bothered her. The press, public opinion... He knew the look of someone who had suffered. But he would not have expected that of the spoiled society princess everyone had described to him.

He had spent his entire journey this morning from Paris to Monte Carlo trawling through her social media and various news articles. To learn about her, not for personal reasons, but in an effort to gauge how he might fix the PR nightmare he'd realised was about to unfold.

There had of course been coverage of her academy successes and the handful of Elite One Premio races she had taken part in as a reserve driver.

But most of the articles he'd seen had focused on a few years in her late teens, most specifically upon a photo shoot she had taken part in a few years back. A rather risqué photo shoot, by most people's standards, and it had shocked him to see that the brand involved was Roux Motors' now defunct luxury car brand.

The New Generation Never Looked So Good! the advert had proudly proclaimed, while showing a fresh-faced, bikini-clad Nina draped over the bonnet of a sleek silver coupe.

The press had taken an interest *'once I was old enough'*, she'd said. Old enough for whom? The girl he'd seen in those photos had looked as though she'd barely finished school. She had come to Paris, to the museum event, incognito, choosing to sneak her way in to confront him rather than using her family name as a bargaining tool. She had asked him to release her from her contract, to allow her to start over elsewhere. None of those actions matched up with the image of her that he'd assumed was accurate.

'Nina…' he said quietly, reaching a hand across the table to grasp hers. 'Could you please try not to look like you're being tortured or blackmailed into having lunch with me?'

She made a non-committal noise, stabbing her fork into her salad. 'I've no idea what you're talking about. I'm having a wonderful time. Thank you so much for giving me the option of having lunch with you in public, Mr Falco.'

'I really think you should call your fiancé by his first name, don't you?' he reminded her, fighting the urge to laugh aloud at the saccharine sweetness in her voice.

'Tristan.' She met his eyes with challenge.

'Can I take that as confirmation that you accept the terms of the deal?' He waited, his hand still extended towards hers across the small table. Slowly, her fingers uncurled from her fork and moved towards his. Her skin was silky soft as she placed her much smaller hand into the palm of his and he wasted no time in closing his grip around hers with triumph.

'I accept,' she said calmly. 'Pending an official contract outlining the details of the arrangement in full.'

He nodded his own agreement, making a mental note to have the terms drawn up immediately. Further conversation was first interrupted by the arrival of their steaks and then subsequently by a business acquaintance who stayed a few moments to arrange a meeting. He was a hard man to pin down, as everyone seemed to say.

When the other man raised a brow in Nina's direction, Tristan made a show of linking his fingers through hers to leave no question as to the nature of their relationship. The media loved a possessive caveman, didn't they? He was simply playing to the cameraman he had seen arrive midway through their food.

That was also why he insisted upon taking her hand as they exited the restaurant terrace and guiding her along the promenade that lined the seafront.

Nina hesitated, glancing anxiously at the slim watch on her wrist. 'I told you I don't have much spare time. I'm racing for the next two weekends until Apollo is ready. I have to get back to headquarters to test out some new strategy in the racing simulation equipment.'

'Surely you want to linger here a few minutes for a prolonged goodbye?' he said smoothly, running a hand along her shoulders as he turned to pull her against him and whisper near her ear. 'Two photographers, just over the wall. Don't look behind you.'

She nodded, seeming to brace herself before relaxing slightly. 'I forgot, sorry. Tell me what you need me to do.'

Tristan closed his eyes against the onslaught of inappropriate thoughts that immediately followed her innocent words.

Think of the deal, Falco. Focus.

'Wrap your arms around my neck and look up at me. Like you can't resist me,' he murmured, sliding a hand tightly around her trim waist. Again, her body tensed before she did some more deep breathing and followed his command. Another woman might have slowly slid her fingertips along his shoulders, teasing him into a sensual haze. Not Nina; she might as well have been performing a Swedish massage, for all the grace she put into her grip. Once she'd settled her hands into place, she met his gaze with an irritated huff. He smiled, a small sound escaping his lips.

Nina instantly tensed up. 'What? Am I doing it wrong?'

His mind tripped over the question, at how odd it seemed for her to be uncertain of something so simple. Surely she had been in a lover's embrace before?

'You're supposed to *melt* into my powerful embrace, not attempt to wring my neck.'

'That doesn't make sense. Humans don't melt,' she argued.

'*Dios.*' Tristan leaned his head forward, pressing his cheek against hers to avoid bursting into laughter at the utter ridiculousness of the situation. 'It just means to bend, to relax into me.'

Nina frowned, turning her face away from him. 'I can't see how anyone will believe we're in the midst of a whirlwind romance when we can't even stand close to one another without arguing.'

'They say intense, combative relationships are often the most passionate.'

'Or the most toxic,' she countered.

'Perhaps.' He pulled her into his arms once more, not missing the slight hitch in her breath as her chest met his. 'Good thing our intensity is all just for show, then, hmm?'

He thought he heard a faint growl under her breath

before she gave in, allowing him to rest her head against his chest while he wrapped his arms around her. With one hand, he moved her hair aside while the other ran a slow path up beneath her leather jacket to stroke along her spine. The thin cotton of her T-shirt was soft beneath his hands, his fingertips tingling as he slowly slid them up and down with measured slowness. She might not have melted, but she certainly relaxed into his touch, her breathing becoming more shallow. She practically vibrated at the caress, her body moulding to his own.

She was like a little cat, he smiled to himself, all claws and teeth until she was stroked into submission. But he barely had a minute to savour his win before she disentangled herself from his grip and they turned to find a mother and her young daughter standing nearby. As Tristan watched in fascination, Nina Roux transformed from the awkward, prickly woman determined to hold him at arm's length to something else entirely. Her voice softened and her eyes sparkled as she spoke to the young girl and signed a number of items with her scrawling autograph.

After a quick chat with the girl's mother about signing up for an upcoming academy open day, they were alone again once more but the haze of their embrace had long gone and been replaced by that same tension he'd felt during their lunch.

Tristan insisted upon driving her back to headquarters, refusing her thinly veiled lie that she needed to walk back on Sophie's orders to make up for missing her afternoon session in the driving simulator.

'Your busy schedule didn't seem to mind a little detour for fan adoration,' he said silkily as the sun-soaked Monte Carlo coast whipped past them.

'I like making time for the kids.' She shrugged. 'They're easier than the adults most of the time.'

'The open day they asked about, it was for a youth academy?'

'The Lola Roux Racing Academy, yes. I founded it a few years back to get more girls into the sport. We have a few training facilities set up around Europe and they do global mobile recruitment drives and scholarships too.' She'd almost forgotten about the upcoming virtual open-day event and quickly opened up her phone to tap a few notes into her schedule.

'A colour-coded schedule. Interesting…'

She looked up to find Tristan's eyes still firmly on the road, but a small smirk on his lips. Feeling self-conscious, she tapped her screen closed. 'Colour-coding makes it easier for me to follow. I like to be organised.'

Truthfully, she *had* to be organised or she didn't function, but she didn't need to tell him all of that. He didn't need to know how she had only two speeds as a professional athlete, workaholic or burnt-out mess. She put a lot of effort into remaining firmly on the working side, so that no one had to see how hard she fell when things came to a stop.

'Do you fund the academy yourself?' he asked a few moments later, spurring her out of her thoughts.

'We originally had support from Roux Racing, but that was cut a couple of years back. It's a big reason why I need to win more races but, for now, yes, I fund it myself.'

He nodded, hands gripping the wheel even tighter. 'You do most things by yourself, from what I can tell.'

'Perhaps I just know that I'm reliable,' she countered.

'And everyone else isn't?'

She remained silent, refusing to rise to the bait of another argument with him. Not when she was still recovering from that embrace on the pier. The way he'd enveloped her in his arms first, then begun stroking her back, and she'd just melted like putty in his hands.

'What about you?' she asked as he brought the car to a stop in front of the gleaming glass façade of the Falco Roux headquarters. 'You seem quite content to run things from afar while you maintain your role of wild playboy. Do you honestly think the media will believe that I've somehow tamed you?'

He turned in his seat until he faced her, midnight-blue eyes sparkling in the late afternoon sun. 'Everything about me is curated; they see what I want them to see. I am in control of the narrative at all times and that is how I prefer it.'

'Does anyone know the real Tristan Falco?'

'Why…do you wish to disassemble me like one of your engines? Find out what makes me tick?'

'I don't care what makes you tick,' she said, inhaling a sharp breath when he leaned forward, placing a kiss upon one cheek then moving slowly to the other side of her face to do the same. A traditional goodbye gesture she'd made herself a thousand times in her life—so why did it feel so intimate with him? The scent of his cologne filled her lungs before she had a chance to defend herself, making her stomach swirl again in that unsettling way it had on the terrace in the Paris museum the night before. He was deliberately disarming her, that was the only explanation for it. He was clearly trying to make this temporary fake fiancée ruse as uncomfortable as possible for her.

'You're getting better at that,' he murmured, pulling away.

'Better at what?'

He smiled, revving the engine loudly to life. 'Lying.'

She schooled her expression so as not to give away how utterly unsettled she felt about everything that had taken place between them in less than twenty-four hours. How on earth was she going to survive another three months like this?

'I'll be in touch about our next date.'

'My schedule is full. As I've said more than once, there is no time.'

'And as I've also said before, you will make time for me.'

His parting words had her grunting and growling the entire climb up the steps to headquarters as she wondered what on earth she had just agreed to.

CHAPTER FIVE

AFTER WRAPPING UP three very successful practice sessions on the first day of the Italian race weekend, Nina had half convinced herself that the previous weekend had been a dream. Despite his threat, Tristan had not been in touch to demand any more of her time, nor had he appeared at the track during any of the press conferences that had taken place yesterday.

Conveniently, their playboy team owner had left Nina alone to issue a litany of *'No comment'* and *'Next question'* after every journalist's probing and snide remarks about the speculation surrounding their public displays of affection.

The Falco Roux team principal was an older man named Jock, a man who already begrudged Nina's presence on the team at all. As predicted, the recent events had only worsened his treatment of her. Her fellow drivers and team members, thankfully, had interjected a couple of times to remind the press that their new team owner had not attended any races yet so far and had very little to do with the day-to-day running of the team. This was after one particularly barbed comment from a news reporter asking if she didn't think her family name had already given her enough privilege in Elite One.

Usually, she shrugged off the overwhelmingly negative opinions of herself as a pay driver, but being accused of using her *body* as a way of climbing the industry ladder felt different. It had got under her skin, making her feel shaky and tight. A feeling that she struggled to throw off, even today on the track as she moved through their strategies and worked on a few last-minute issues with the car.

She had seen the other team drivers and crew looking at her and whispering when they thought she wasn't looking. It didn't take much to imagine what they might be thinking. Despite the overwhelmingly positive public reaction to the romance, from a professional point of view, some people were uncomfortable with the notion. Billionaire playboy or not, Tristan was older than her by twelve years and he was essentially her boss. And despite his assurances that he would swing the narrative, Tristan had done nothing to protect her from the backlash so far. On the contrary, he'd practically fed her to the wolves.

Friday of the race weekends was often a strange mix of on-track and off-track commitments, followed by whatever events and public appearances were required of her in the evening. She took her time showering in her modest hotel suite, taking advantage of the sleek high-pressure shower and steam room to try to blast away some of her stress. She didn't have a high-maintenance beauty regime by any standards, but as she took in her reflection in the mirror, she had a feeling that her usual routine of moisturiser and mascara wasn't going to be enough to mask the sheer exhaustion on her face.

At least the cocktail dress the PR team had sent up was a delightfully lightweight and comfortable satin stretch material that wouldn't irritate her skin for the entire evening. She couldn't avoid heels, but compromised by sliding a pair of simple black flats into her clutch for when the discomfort became too much and she could slip away. Which she fully intended to do as early as possible.

There were three events on the roster from what she could remember, a charity meet and greet, a dinner with their Italian investors, the Marchesi family, followed by a rooftop cocktail hour and dancing.

With the track qualifying sessions beginning tomorrow, it was accepted that the drivers could leave at their own discretion once their minimum appearance had been made. Appearances meant photographs, lots and lots of them—and as far as she knew, Tristan Falco was still in hiding. Perhaps she'd imagined the entire debacle at the beginning of the week, or perhaps he'd taken her advice and realised that she was far more trouble than she was worth. That a match between the two of them would never convince anyone.

Perhaps he'd simply found someone else to fulfil his temporary fiancée needs. Perhaps she was about to be fired, after all. Her stomach tightened at the thought.

Her security guards escorted her in the lift down to where a sleek limo awaited her outside, a much more extravagant ride than she was used to being assigned. Her curiosity was short-lived, however, as the door opened when she was a few steps away and out emerged the object of her thoughts.

Tristan Falco had come to Milan after all, and that meant the deal was still on. She didn't know whether the sudden tightening in her stomach was from fear or anticipation as he leaned forward to place a kiss upon her right cheek. Again, the smell of his cologne was surprisingly pleasant, as was the weight of his hand upon her waist as he looked down at her.

'Miss me?' he asked.

'It's been five days.'

'You poor thing, you've kept count.' The tilt of his head and slight smirk to anyone else might seem like a gentle lovers' back-and-forth. No one looking on would know that Nina was desperately resisting the urge to smack him in the face.

'If I were to keep count of how many race weekends you've actually attended, I wouldn't need to go further than my thumb. That is, if you actually plan to attend the race.'

'After the spike in sales this week, I'm under strict instruction from Astrid Lewis not to miss a single race weekend for the rest of the season.'

Of course, he wasn't here to watch her race or cheer her on or anything of the sort. His appearance here was entirely to do with the optics of this nonsensical PR stunt his team was executing. Apart from the speculation around their relationship, the other main news point in the motorsports world was Apollo's decision to return to Elite One for his family's rival team. It was an action that no team had ever seen in the past, a driver bearing the name of a historic team signing for their family's biggest rival.

Of course, no one was talking about the fact that Nina had spent four days this week with the team as they began the monumental task of readying their new driver for the second half of the season. With the Belgian Premio next weekend, followed by Spain the weekend after, and then the three-week summer break, Apollo's first race would be a historic one, starting as it was with the revival of the Argentinian Elite One Premio in Buenos Aires. She doubted that Astrid had to coerce Tristan to attend *that* race.

'I know I haven't been around anywhere near enough. Thankfully I have my beautiful fiancée to step up now and give me all the harsh truths I've needed to hear.'

'I wasn't trying to be harsh.'

'I know,' he said with a slight smile. 'It took a moment for me to realise that; it's just your nature to be rather...'

'Blunt?' she offered defensively.

'I was going to say boldly honest,' he said, his gaze holding onto hers for a long moment before he continued. 'I'm not here to fight. I'm actually here to take care of some very important business.'

Nina looked out of the window as the car slowed. They were in the very heart of Milan where some of the most expensive and grand fashion houses had their flagship stores. The limousine pulled to a stop outside an ornate historic-looking triple-storey store, one that bore the Falco crest.

'We are not here for me, Nina, we are here for you,' Tristan said once they were inside.

'Me?'

'I hope you don't mind but when we planned tonight's look, I specifically told the team to leave out jewellery for this reason.'

Nina stilled. 'You planned my...wait, you're choosing my clothing now as well?'

'Your personal trainer Sophie was kind enough to give me some guidance on your rather specific taste in clothing. The material is to your liking, no?'

He had picked out her dress. Suddenly the silken slide of the material against her thighs as they walked along the central aisle of the cavernous store felt intimate and seductive, rather than comforting. Much like the man himself. There was nothing about Tristan Falco that was comforting at all.

'So you're here to drape me in your diamonds like a walking advertisement, is that it?'

'Actually, we're here for a ring. Your engagement ring, to be precise.'

If Nina had been a cartoon character, she was pretty sure this would be the moment when her jaw would drop comically to the floor. As it was, she just about managed to keep herself from tripping over her own shoes. Had he picked out the damned heels as well?

'I thought... I assumed that we wouldn't be announcing that part so soon.'

'We won't be announcing anything. You'll be seen tonight wearing an appropriately eye-catching diamond on your left hand. Gossip will do the rest.' He waited a beat, his eyes searching her face with a frown. 'You look surprised, *cariña*. Surely you didn't expect the CEO of

Falco Diamonds' fiancée to walk around without a gigantic rock on her finger?'

'No, I suppose not,' she murmured, her fingertips suddenly feeling tingly and numb as she fought not to twist them in her lap. Her mother had taught her, forced her not to fidget when she was uneasy or nervous. She'd learned how to keep her breathing even and steady, how to periodically meet the gaze of important people so that she didn't seem shifty or untrustworthy. But she had never been trained how to respond in a situation like this.

As she sat frozen still, the world's most untameable bachelor slid a tray of antique diamond rings in front of her. In her peripheral vision, the store manager and sales assistant looked on with whimsical smiles as though they were observing a truly romantic moment between a couple in love. She supposed that was why Tristan reached over and grabbed her hand gently, sliding his thumb across her knuckles and leaning forward to move a lock of hair from her forehead.

'I asked them to bring this one up from the vault.' He held up a small red box, separate from the tray of glittering pieces the manager had placed between them. The box snapped open, revealing a truly gigantic black diamond surrounded by a coronet of brilliant white gemstones. 'But you are the one who must wear it, after all. So take your pick from everything you see here.'

She hardly remembered what she did next, but one moment Tristan was smiling with triumph and the next he was on one knee before her. He slid the black diamond ring slowly onto her finger while a gentle round of applause sounded out from their small audience.

'Perfect,' he murmured, meeting her eyes for one scorching second before turning to ask someone to bring a tray of earrings and necklaces to match her newest accessory.

He insisted upon draping the jewels around her neck himself. With the mirror in front of her, she watched as he slid her hair to one side and did up the clasp at the back of her necklace. His eyes met hers with a silent question through the reflection in the mirror. Nina glanced at him, then quickly away as her breathing began to feel a little tight.

To all the world right now, she had just become the future Mrs Falco, and she couldn't even look her fiancé in the eye without having a mild panic attack. What on earth would she do when he eventually had to kiss her again?

Tristan could not say that he had ever imagined how a proposal of his own would go, but this certainly had not been it. Nina had looked as though she was breathing through a rather painful dental procedure during their entire ring selection, elevating into a mild state of frozen panic once he had actually placed the diamond upon her finger. Things had not improved much since they'd made their way out of the jewellery store to pose briefly for a small crowd of photographers. Nina had brushed her hair out of her face with her left hand as he'd instructed her to, and they had travelled to their first event of the evening in silence. He lost sight of her soon after arriving at the charity event, with his presence being required for a series of minor television interviews and hers for an Elite One photo call with the other drivers.

His own interviews were predictably focused on getting him to release any details about his relationship with Nina, which he handled with ease, taking enjoyment out of toying with his word selection. His team had not had to coach him much on the art of selective information sharing; Tristan had always viewed his relationship with the press as a game of sorts, a series of chess moves, using them as he pleased. It had worked in his favour so far, but when he'd seen some of the articles and social media posts that had been released about Nina during the few days since their scandal had gone public, he'd immediately booked for his private train car to take him from Paris to Milan.

Even now, not knowing where she was or what questions she was having to field alone made him feel like the world's biggest jerk. He'd played it cool, but sharing more than he'd intended during their last encounter had made him feel off balance, and so he had done something he never usually did. He'd ghosted her.

It wouldn't happen again. From this moment on, he intended for them to act as a team, whether she liked it or not.

Teamwork seemed to be a concept that Nina was quite familiar with, judging by her current cosy pose with her co-driver, Daniele Roberts. The Scottish-Italian heartthrob had been one of their team's biggest assets over the past year, and Tristan knew Nina had played an expert game in defending him into first position in a race earlier in the season, when their lead driver had been unwell. Tristan might not have attended that race either but he had kept tabs on the results and highlights, as he had done for every other racing weekend this year. As he watched, Roberts leaned in and whispered something into Nina's ear, making her laugh loudly before she composed herself back into a serene smiling position for the camera. Once the photographer had finished up, she turned back to Roberts, lightly punching him on the arm.

Their interaction was so friendly, so *easy*, it caught Tristan off guard. She wasn't cranky with the other man, nor was she picking apart his words or studiously avoiding his gaze. In fact, she seemed to be actively enjoying their conversation as the two moved to the side of the room seeking a more private spot.

He immediately felt his body tense as if to launch into pursuit, but before he could he was interrupted by a familiar bellowing Italian voice. Valerio Marchesi had once been his biggest rival when they had both attended boarding school, a rivalry that had lasted until they had bonded over their shared traumatic experiences and Tristan had eagerly helped the other man to access some therapy and begin to heal. That healing, along with some other, more shady and dramatic occurrences, had led to Valerio marrying Daniela Avelar, who stepped up now to give Tristan a familiar kiss on the cheek.

'I heard the most delicious rumour this week, Falco,' Valerio said, a mischievous smile lighting up his face as he slid onto a barstool alongside him and demanded the full details of how Tristan had gone from a devoted bachelor to being engaged to a racing-car driver all in a matter of a few days.

'It seems your fiancée is a little busy at present,' Valerio said wryly, glancing at the spot where Tristan was very much still keeping tabs on Nina and her teammate. 'I do love to see you finally getting your comeuppance.'

He was vaguely aware of the fact that his friend referenced a night in the past, where his wife had asked Tristan to play the role of her date to prove a point. A night that felt like a lifetime ago now that Valerio and Dani were very happily married with two children. But he didn't have time to rehash the past, not when his fiancée was being pulled into a deep embrace by a twinkly eyed dandy in plain view of the entire room.

His friends' laughter quickly blended into the background noise as Tristan made his way across the gallery towards where Nina and the other man had retreated. As he got within earshot he heard the Scot ask, 'So you're not even sleeping together yet?'

Tristan's blood boiled as he crossed the rest of the distance between them with two long strides. Feeling a hint of satisfaction as Roberts's smirking expression faltered when he caught sight of Tristan standing over Nina's shoulder.

'That seems like a very personal question, Mr Roberts.' Tristan smiled wolfishly, leaning down to press a lingering kiss upon Nina's bare shoulder before sliding a hand around her waist and meeting the other man's eyes. Instead of looking shaken or uncomfortable, Roberts seemed only to smile wider.

'It's just locker-room banter,' he said, his trademark

broad grin pasted upon his handsome face. The driver's playboy reputation rivalled even Tristan's own if the tabloids were true. But Tristan had always liked Roberts's upbeat charisma, until this very moment in fact. Because right now he wanted to wipe that smile right off his face.

'You like to be treated like one of the guys, isn't that right, Roux?' Roberts said.

Nina let out a small huff of laughter, at the same time attempting to subtly slide her waist out of Tristan's grip. He held on even tighter, splaying his hand across her abdomen and noting that his finger-span almost covered her from hip to hip. Below the belt, his body reacted primitively to that knowledge, but above the belt he remained stony-faced and focused on staring down the man who seemed intent on challenging his patience.

Nina sucked in a swift breath and looked up at him for a split second before turning back to answer Roberts. 'I think we both know I am far superior to all of you, but yes, the banter is fine.'

'Well, she's *not* one of the guys. She's my fiancée.' Tristan offered a charming smile of his own, through rather clenched teeth. 'And I take offence to you probing for the intimate details of our relationship.'

'He wasn't probing about our intimate details,' Nina said drily. 'He was just probing about yours. He's quite curious about your bedroom prowess, it seems. That's actually been the most common question I've been asked this week. Is it true that Tristan Falco is a magician in the bedroom?'

Tristan choked. 'A magician now, is it? Last I heard

I'd been compared to a deity. I've been downgraded, it seems.'

Roberts laughed aloud and then had the good sense to slowly retreat from their conversation. Leaving them alone in the corner of the gallery.

'I don't think the caveman performance is quite necessary for this ruse to work, do you?' Nina turned from him and surveyed the crowd in the gallery below.

'I believe I was pretty clear that I would be the one to decide what is necessary.'

'Ah yes, how silly of me to forget. I have simply to endure your brooding looks and act as a walking jewellery stand.' She sighed, her eyes lingering for a moment longer than necessary upon the area below his belt buckle. 'I should have assured Roberts that there is no chance of me ever experiencing the truth behind those rumours of your...prowess.'

Tristan froze, not quite believing his ears. Surely he had misheard her, or misconstrued her intention. Surely she couldn't mean...?

'Deity...' she mused thoughtfully. 'It's like everyone is asking me about the supercar parked in my garage, and I'm expected to brag...even though I'm not allowed to drive it.'

Tristan startled. 'Nina...what are you—'

'Oh, relax, I'm not actually propositioning you, Tristan. No doubt my brother has already warned you off too.'

'Your brother has no say in who I do or do not take to bed.'

'Well, *he* thinks he does.' She wandered to the next

painting, her gaze roaming over the paint strokes absently as her voice tightened with a hint of emotion. 'He hasn't spoken to me in fourteen months, did you know that? Then today I saw he'd left me a voicemail, no apology or explanation, just warning me not to sleep with you.'

Tristan ignored the pang of guilt in his gut at the knowledge that he alone knew the truth of why her brother had left her alone for that long. But he couldn't tell her yet…and how very unfair that was—for both of them. All Tristan could hope was that when Nina did finally discover the truth about what he'd done, she'd see that Tristan had acted in the Roux company's best interests and understand the reason for his silence. Instead he simply said, 'He's just being protective of you.'

'He used to be,' she said, turning to face him once more. 'I only wish he was half as protective of our family's legacy and my inheritance as he is over my virtue.'

Tristan laughed at the outdated term. 'Your virtue? You make it sound as though I'm some kind of devilish rake and you're an innocent debutante.'

A strange look came over her face, and she took a few steps away, looking up at a nearby painting. 'My reputation is my virtue, I suppose. Just look how easily people assume that I must be some kind of calculating seductress, because I've managed to pin down the world's most untameable bachelor.'

'I suppose that makes me the devil in this scenario?' He paused, realising he didn't like that contrast between them one bit. 'Are you wondering if I plan to seduce you, Nina?'

'Are you?' Her eyes pinned his without missing a beat, holding him captive with their unfathomable depths that seemed to always see far too much.

He made a weak attempt at charm. 'What would you do if I said yes?'

She shrugged. 'I walked away easily enough after your first attempt.'

Whatever he'd expected her answer to be, it wasn't that. Ignoring the now persistent ache below his belt at the turn this conversation had taken, Tristan leaned back against the balcony rail and surveyed his pint-sized fake fiancée. There was no trace of mirth in her delicate features, nor any indication that she might be testing him or making fun of him. She was absolutely serious. He was struck suddenly by how young she was. And how old and jaded he felt in comparison. He'd flirted and toyed with plenty of women in his life, but with her... it wasn't the same. There was no guile in her words, no double entendre or expectation.

Having her look at him this way... It made him feel as though he'd had his clothing peeled off piece by piece, leaving him with nowhere to hide. It irritated him that she could influence him with so little effort. It wouldn't do.

'Are you challenging me, *cariña*?'

'Of course, you would see it that way. Your reputation precedes you on such a scale it borders upon a cult. I'd be lying if I said I wasn't curious to see if any of it is true or if it's just more of your...*spin*.'

'You believe that I've hired women to stalk me and break into my hotel rooms on purpose?'

'No.' She paused, thoughtful for a moment. 'But I believe you do nothing to discourage it. If this were a real relationship, I would never have a moment's peace.'

'If this were a real relationship, I'd make sure you only felt peace. You'd be so relaxed you'd practically float from my bed, out into the world.' He let his voice drop to a murmur as he fought not to step closer.

Her pupils dilated, a slight blush appearing high on her cheeks. She opened her mouth to respond, then closed it and looked meekly away as they were called to rejoin the party for more photos. Tristan felt a thrum of satisfaction rush through him. His little cat might play tough, but she wasn't unaffected by him. Not at all.

CHAPTER SIX

Tristan was not present at the Belgian Premio events the following weekend, nor did he show up for Apollo Accardi's first official training sessions in their Monaco headquarters over the week that followed. Nina threw herself into her own training, determined to finish out her last stint as second driver in Barcelona with her head held high.

Her agent had contacted her this morning with the news that representatives from Accardi Autosport were seeking a new driver for next year's season now that their long-time champion was retiring. She'd hesitated but told them to put her name out there. When her deal with Tristan was concluded, she'd be out of contract at the end of this season after all, so she needed to keep her options open.

But the guilt weighed heavily on her mind as her team smiled and joked while they gathered at the marina to travel from Monte Carlo to Barcelona. They'd been treated to a night on a Velamar superyacht, likely courtesy of their main sponsor as a thank-you for their fantastic result in Italy. Of course, the vessel they were directed to was the largest one in the bay, a world-famous superyacht design that she remembered was called *La Sirinetta II*, but a different name was pasted on the bow of this one.

The Falco Experience.

Tristan appeared on the welcome deck dressed casually in a pair of tan linen trousers and an open-collared polo shirt. He greeted each of the team by name, leaving her for last as everyone else hustled to get on board and find their room for the night. The ship was huge and had more than enough bedrooms for them all, but, still, she was amazed that he'd so easily decided to open up his precious vessel to them all. It wasn't usual for the team owner and drivers to travel along with the mechanics and administrative staff, but then again not much about Tristan's ownership had been traditional so far.

The team was awash with excitement as they were greeted with fruity cocktails and canapés while Tristan played gracious host. After he greeted her with little more than a quick peck on her cheek and then instructed her to continue on to her guests, Nina quickly realised that he intended to keep the distance between them.

It shouldn't have bothered her that he'd become so distant again after their night of flirtation in Milan. She'd all but dared him to seduce her after all, hadn't she? Sure, she'd tried to pass it off as casual flirtation but she knew better than anyone that she was utterly terrible at lying. She'd thought about being seduced by Tristan Falco more times in the past three weeks than she'd ever dare to admit. Thinking of him had become some kind of sickness, affecting her focus on the track and infiltrating her very steamy dreams at night like a constant itch that she was forbidden to scratch.

She'd always hated being told that things were forbidden. It was rather like placing a giant flashing button within her reach emblazoned with bright letters that commanded: Do Not Touch—even though she was a dedicated rule follower by nature, all she wanted to do was touch it.

She knew that when he'd first proposed this deal, he'd said it would be safer for them both to keep their arrangement platonic behind closed doors. But deep down, she didn't truly believe that was the reason he'd shown no sign of wanting more once the cameras panned away and it was just the two of them. Apart from the fact that she was a driver on the team he owned, she knew that aesthetically she was miles away from the kind of women she'd seen draped on his arms at that event in Paris. She wasn't tall or willowy, she didn't laugh prettily at his jokes and compliment him on his charms.

Once again...she was too much.

Determined not to allow him to see how self-conscious that realisation made her feel, she focused on chatting with her team and smiled when Astrid Lewis appeared to greet her. Astrid's appearance at social events had become more and more rare lately. Her son, Luca, was an expert in everything Elite One and had never missed a single race until he'd started school last autumn. Nina had spent some time with them in their home in London before the season started and discovered that Luca had been diagnosed with autism. This had stunned her because of how often in the past Astrid had compared her sensitive, serious little boy to Nina herself. Nina had always felt a deep connection to Luca, and knowing more details about how he experienced the world only made her love him more.

But when Astrid had gently suggested that Nina perhaps should look into the experiences of some late identified autistic adults she'd found online, the moment had become a little awkward between them. It had played heavily on her mind since, but she shook off the memory and embraced her friend.

'Please tell me you're not here to add to my schedule,' Nina asked quickly. Every time Astrid approached her with an eerily calm look in place it usually accompanied bad news of some sort.

'Tristan said he told you about the Falco Diamonds centenary campaign that was in the works?'

Nina fought the urge to groan. 'Yes, I remember.'

'The actual campaign will be shot in Buenos Aires next month, but the PR team wanted to go ahead and do some tests while you're at your photo shoot in Barcelona this week.'

Nina frowned, remembering that she was scheduled to shoot as a cover model for a magazine. 'Do they want to do this at the same time as the shoot?'

'That's up to you, I would say perhaps all together might suit better with how much energy these things take from you. But here's the thing… The magazine got wind of all of this and now they want to include recent events in the narrative. More specifically, they want to involve Tristan.'

As if summoned by his name, Tristan appeared at Nina's

side with two flutes of champagne in hand and offered her one. 'Who wishes to involve me and in what?'

Astrid quickly went through the proposed feature from a prominent sports and fitness magazine that had shown interest in featuring women in motorsport and using Nina as their cover star.

'This all sounds excellent, but I don't see why I would be needed.' Tristan frowned. 'Unless you mean they wish to use some Falco pieces as part of the shoot?'

'I definitely want us to include Falco Diamonds in some way, to really emphasise that connection between the two brands. I think it's a great idea to push a united image for people to see. We also need to find a suitable location on short notice. But what I really wanted to ask was… They wanted to see if you'd consider taking the photos yourself, Tristan,' Astrid said.

'Absolutely not.' Tristan's face tightened. 'I'm sorry to disappoint there. But the location and the diamonds, I can arrange. I've been meaning to check in on my uncle's estate while we're here anyway. He left it to me, rather than my cousin, Victor. My uncle was more like a father to me, and I think he knew I'd preserve it just as he wanted. He had a classic car collection that would work well as a backdrop.'

Nina felt the tension coming off him in waves as Astrid walked away, leaving them both alone. She took a sip of champagne. 'I didn't know you were a photographer.'

'Briefly…a very long time ago. After my uncle's untimely death I travelled for a while. I dabbled in portrait photography and published some work in a few magazines under a pseudonym.'

She saw the flash of pain in his eyes at the mention of his uncle, and thought of him, travelling the world in his grief and finding beauty where he could. 'You don't take photos any more?'

'No,' he said simply. 'Not in the past few years anyway. I still have most of my equipment but… I just don't have the time any more.'

'One should always make time for hobbies you enjoy. Or do you only think of finding pleasure in bed these days?'

He smirked. 'We've barely been alone for three minutes and you've already mentioned my sex life. That must be a new record. You truly are obsessed.'

'That's probably accurate,' she muttered under her breath.

'What was that?'

'Nothing… I was just thinking…you *should* shoot the photos yourself,' she blurted, immediately regretting her words when his eyes flashed a warning at her. He shook his head, downing the rest of his champagne flute in one mouthful.

'It's just an idea.' Nina shrugged one shoulder. 'Astrid is very observant, and she knows that I'm usually quite awkward about these things. It might help to not have a stranger behind the lens.'

'Nice to know I'm not a stranger now at least.' He smirked. 'But no, I have to be back in Paris once the race is through. It's a prominent magazine, they will have a reputable photographer in charge. You'll be fine.'

She nodded. 'Makes sense that you plan to leave so quickly.'

'Makes sense how exactly?'

'Well, after I expressed my curiosity in Milan… You've kept your distance.'

'Perhaps I've just been busy.'

'You were flirtatious, until I mentioned that I was not entirely opposed to exploring the attraction between us and then you backed off.'

'Nina…'

'Don't worry, I'm not about to express the same interest again. I have some self-respect, Tristan. It's just infuriating dealing with people's assumptions about me. When the truth is utterly laughable.'

'The truth?'

'The media have gone from painting me as an ice queen to wondering if I am some kind of secret sex goddess because I've "pinned you down".'

His eyes darkened and he muttered hoarsely, 'A sex goddess?'

'It's the natural fit for a man described as a deity in the bedroom, no?'

'Sounds like a match made in heaven.'

Nina rolled her eyes, turning to brace her hands against the railing and look out to where the sun was beginning to dip against the horizon, turning the water a beautiful mixture of orange and yellow. She was aware of Tristan moving closer behind her, but, still, her breath caught when she felt his arm brush against hers. He wasn't touching her, but he wasn't exactly keeping his distance either. Her skin thrummed in response and she fought the urge to remain still.

'You believe that me keeping my distance means that I was turned off by your honesty?'

'Weren't you?'

A low chuckle escaped his lips and she saw him shake his head gently in her peripheral vision. 'I find your honesty to be the single most entrancing thing that I've encountered in recent memory, Nina Roux.'

She inhaled a soft breath as he moved closer, his eyes raking down over her skin in a look so scorching hot he might as well have been undressing her with his hands.

'You think I don't want you?' he murmured. 'You think that I don't obsess over all the reasons that I want to touch you? And all the reasons why giving in to that impulse would ruin us both?'

'But…why?'

'Apart from you being twelve years younger than me, and the fact that I'm technically your boss, I pulled you into this ridiculous deal in the first place, dangling your freedom from your contract in front of you. For me to seduce you would be taking advantage of you.'

She found she wasn't bothered by the age gap or the fact that he was her boss. 'What if I wanted to be seduced? Is that against your rules?'

'Nina…' he warned.

She moved closer, testing him by reaching up to place both of her hands on his shoulders. He could move away if he wished, or he could tell her no. But the burning desire she could see in his eyes told her that he wouldn't do either of those things. Feeling emboldened, she reached up and was delighted when he immediately lowered his head to hers in response. He let her control the kiss, making himself pliable under her hands and lips as she explored him. He tasted just as delicious as she remembered, the sensations of the breeze upon her hair and his hands snaking around her waist to pull her closer against his hard body were like heaven. She heard a moan, and realised it came from her own throat.

Kissing Tristan again was as explosive as she knew it would be. It was the kind of feeling she usually got only when driving full throttle around the track, as if she were flying through the air. It made her stomach twirl and her thoughts turn blank. All she could feel was him, all she could think about was how it felt and how badly she wanted more.

So much more.

He pressed her back against the railings, pressing himself against her, and she could feel the hard ridge of his erection against her abdomen. She was wearing jeans, and he was wearing linen trousers, but still the intimacy was almost too much for her. They might as well have been completely naked for all she knew, the way her insides turned to molten fire, and she ground back against him.

Her sensual movements made his body harden even further against hers, and she heard a low growl in his throat as he speared his fingers through her hair and took control of the kiss, deepening it and taking her just as she wished to be taken. This was what she needed, exactly this.

Too late, she heard footsteps coming down the steps and they paused just in time to see Astrid's shocked face before the woman turned and quickly exited the way she'd come.

Nina pressed both hands against her face, groaning. 'Oh, my God, did that just happen? She's seen us.'

'She did,' Tristan said, standing up to his full height and putting some distance between them.

'It's okay, everyone else thinks that we're engaged anyway. Of course, Astrid knows the truth, but I doubt she'll make a big deal of it.'

'That's not why I'm annoyed right now, Nina,' Tristan said. 'Every time I am alone with you, I lose control. It's not acceptable. I never lose control. We set parameters for this arrangement and you…keep pushing.'

'You're right. I deliberately pushed those parameters. And I won't apologise for that,' she said defiantly.

'You won't?' he asked, raising an eyebrow.

Nina's heartbeat fluttered at the heat still evident in Tristan's gaze. 'No. I'm very attracted to you and I was curious.'

'Damn it.' He moved closer, licking his lips as he stared down at her. 'Damn *you* with your curiosity and your refusal to accept the word no.'

'If you had actually said no at any point during the past ten minutes I would have stopped,' she said as sweetly as she could manage.

'Hell would have a better chance of freezing over, kitten.' He was upon her again, his lips crushing hers against his as he pulled her close and kissed her senseless once more. Until she was breathless and aching between her thighs.

'I only have so much willpower, Nina. Are you sure this is what you want?' He growled the words in between kisses.

'Yes.' She moaned against his plundering mouth, gasping as he stroked her sensitive nipples through the material of her bra and T-shirt. She felt as though she'd played with fire and now she was getting an up-close-and-personal demonstration of what it felt like to go up in flames. His hands explored her willing body inch by inch, his mouth not breaking their kiss. But when his fingers began to toy with the top button of her jeans, Nina felt the first flicker of uncertainty freeze her up. Of course Tristan noticed the moment she stopped enthusiastically kissing him back.

'Sorry, I got carried away.' he murmured. 'Maybe we should take this somewhere more private?'

Nina shook her head, feeling reality come crashing back with all the subtlety of a cold bracing shower. She was on his yacht, with their entire team nearby. Plus, even if she did throw caution to the wind and go back to his bedroom with him, after all her talk tonight of seducing him, he would be expecting her to be experienced. Not a nervous virgin who had absolutely no idea what she was doing.

'Can we pause for a moment?' she asked quietly.

He nodded, taking a step back as if needing that physical distance between them in order to bring his desire under control. The knowledge that he wanted her just as badly as she wanted him was a heady kind of power that made her feel alight with passion.

'I want this. Very much,' she assured him a little nervously. 'It's just…a little fast for me. Also, this weekend is really important and I can hardly focus around you as it is.'

'Are you saying I'm jeopardising your race? I'm very flattered.'

'Of course you are. But yes, I think perhaps we should pause this…until afterwards?'

'Only if you promise to schedule me into your diary at the earliest opportunity,' he murmured against her cheek. 'In bright red pen. I don't know why, but I'm rather obsessed with your colour-coding.'

She smiled, feeling a blush in her cheeks. 'For the next three days my focus is on the race, but after that I'm yours.'

The moment she spoke the words, he froze, his hands tightening upon her waist for a split second. 'Cristo, you could drive a man wild saying things like that.'

She hadn't intended to drive him wild, but if the consequence of speaking honestly was him kissing her like this, she'd continue to give her thoughts free rein. 'I feel like I should be honest that, um… I don't usually do this. Like, I've never—'

He continued to kiss a trail down the side of her neck, so she wasn't entirely sure if he'd heard her. A series of low murmurs was all he said in response.

'Let's get you to bed, Nina. Before I'm tempted to tuck you in myself.'

He walked her to her bedroom door and lingered for a long moment, one hand braced quite attractively on the doorjamb as he stared down at her with possession. 'Three days,' he repeated.

'Three days.' She nodded.

The executive box of the Spanish Premio was filled predictably with people that Tristan did not know. He knew of them, of course, politicians and celebrities schmoozing with one another in the hopes of gaining influence. Likely some of them might actually follow the sport, but Elite One race weekends were as much about the experience and atmosphere as the racing after all. He'd deliberately procured a spot near the back of the room, away from the windows, once the race had begun an hour ago.

Even after years of therapy following the aeroplane accident that had killed his uncle and almost killed him too, the sound of roaring engines still managed to set his teeth on edge. But he was managing it, as he always did. He was a master of the public performance, after all, his guests simply seeing their bored owner schmoozing and wishing he were anywhere but here. No one knew the truth was that the very idea of Nina whizzing around that track at such high speeds was almost more than he could bear.

She would laugh, of course, if she knew that he held her skill in complete regard and truly hoped that all of her dreams on the track would come true...if only it didn't involve actually putting her life in the hands of a car.

The car was in great shape, and according to the mechanics on the team downstairs their strategy was sound and both of their drivers were in fighting form, as was evidenced by their current positions in fourth and fifth place out of twenty.

The Accardi team were in first and second, and had been for most of the race, but Nina's expert defending and Roberts's aggressive driving style had already moved them through several impressive overtakes. As he listened to the commentary he heard them each move up another spot.

'Do my eyes deceive me?' a British voice sounded out and Tristan looked up to see Astrid's smiling face approaching him. 'Tristan Falco, in the flesh at a race weekend. Don't tell me you're actually following my advice.'

'Actually it was Nina who convinced me that I was actively impeding growth by not showing my full support to the team.'

Astrid smirked. 'Yes, I noticed she seems to have made *quite* the impression on you.'

Tristan cleared his throat, tugging at his suddenly tight collar as Astrid continued to give him an all too knowing look.

'You know, Tristan, I wasn't quite sure at first if this plan would work but the narrative in the media has felt like a real romance. You're doing a great job of making it look that way anyway. Even in private, it's quite the dedication to the cause you're both showing. Just…be careful with her, okay?'

Tristan thought of Nina's hesitancy three weeks ago when she'd agreed to this deal, how he'd insisted he wouldn't allow the lines between them to become blurred. How he'd been so confident in assuring her that everything between them was just for show. The trouble was, the more time they spent alone, the more they both seemed to forget. Or at least their bodies did anyway.

The attraction he felt to her was like nothing he'd ever experienced before. It was all-consuming, bordering upon an obsession at times, and he'd even found himself checking in on her at training or showing up at her hotel to take her for lunch over the past few days. She had taken it all in her stride, of course, giving him no indication of how she truly felt. But still, her words on the yacht had stuck with him.

'My focus is on the race, but after that I'm yours.'

She hadn't meant it in the way that his primitive brain had taken it. That she would be *his*. That he would possess her, finally. But to all intents and purposes, she would be in his bed at least. He fought to control the sudden reaction as his body got tighter.

'I heard an interesting rumour,' Astrid said, reminding him of where he was and helping him to refocus his thoughts.

'A good one, I hope.'

'An important one, for sure… Accardi have their eyes on Nina.'

Tristan paused with his glass midway to his mouth, his eyes snapping up to focus on his PR manager. 'Over my dead body.'

Astrid pursed her lips, tilting her head at his rather emotional reaction. 'I thought you might feel that way. But, as it stands, under the terms of your agreement with her, you're going to free her from her contract at the end of the season, aren't you?'

'Yes, but they don't know that.'

'Are you planning to keep her, Tristan?' Astrid asked, her bespectacled gaze as shrewd as ever. 'Because after the decisions made by this team in the past month, I don't think Nina is planning to stay.'

'That's not the point. The point is that this is blatant

retaliation by Enzo Accardi for us signing his grandson. And he is not going to use Nina as a weapon to play games with me.'

'You do realise this is Elite One, yes? The most game-playing of all the motorsports. It's all drama, Tristan. The racing only takes up five per cent of the entertainment. Nina wants to leave anyway and just think of the media storm that would follow.'

He knew Enzo Accardi, and he also knew the stories about the old man and how lecherous he was, how ruthless and underhanded. There was a good reason why Apollo had refused to ever race for him again. To think that Enzo might get his hands on Nina... To think what kind of hoops he might require her to jump through in order for her to achieve her dreams...

Suddenly he realised the decision to pass Nina over in favour of signing a much more experienced driver for the remainder of this season had been completely the wrong call. He'd thought he'd been doing the right thing for the team, but he could see now with gut-churning guilt and horror that this should have been Nina's season with her team, and they were practically allowing their biggest asset to walk into the arms of their vilest competitor. Despite it being an obvious retaliation on Enzo's part, the senior Accardi would not be pursuing Nina for his team if she weren't also one of the most prominent rising stars on the track. All he could hope was that his mistake wouldn't prove too costly—for Nina, for the team...and for himself. He knew now that her skill was practically unmatched, along with her even, cool temperament. If she'd been in the number one Falco Roux seat today, she would already have been ahead, but she continued to stay behind their primary driver, defending him and allowing him to rush towards victory.

As he listened, the crowd went wild as a commentator announced Roberts overtaking into second place right behind Accardi's number one driver. Unable to look away, he moved closer to a nearby monitor and watched as the cameraman zoomed in on where Nina and Accardi's number two driver were now battling it out for third place. His whole body tight as a string, he watched as she edged and weaved behind the other driver as they both hurtled in the rain towards the next turn much too fast.

No! Surely she wasn't planning to... Tristan fought the urge to shout at the screen, controlling his own panicked reaction. But hell, it was a hairpin band on a downhill slant, and surely it was impossible to keep the car under control... But he watched as, to his amazement, Nina feinted in one direction and then, in a move so skilled and sleek the entire crowd gasped, she slid neatly between the other car and the apex of the track to steal neatly into third place.

He was by no means an expert in motorsport, but whatever that was, it was pure poetry in motion. The woman had a gift. A smile transformed his face and he couldn't help a bellow escaping his chest as he cheered along with the rest of the garage. It was the final lap, and all going well they would have two team members on the podium for the first time. The first time in fifteen years, the commentator announced wildly.

Tristan turned to their team principal, slapping the

man on the back and listening as the R & D team continued to monitor their drivers and ensure they kept their positions towards the finish line.

But as Nina pushed to the max around the final lap, the Accardi driver behind her gained pace and grew reckless. Disaster came swift and ruthlessly, as it often did. One touch of his front wing against Nina's rear tyre was all it took, sending both cars into a helpless spin.

'No! I've lost it, I've lost it.'

Her frantic voice was the last thing Tristan heard as her car hydroplaned at speed before careening into the wall.

CHAPTER SEVEN

THE MEDICAL TEAM was quick and efficient as usual in tending to the minor bruising that Nina had incurred when the other driver had hit the back of her car. Incidents of any kind were treated with severity in Elite One, a sport that prided itself on the huge safety improvements they had developed for drivers and crew over the past couple of decades. In no time at all she'd been signed off to return to her hotel, accompanied by her trainer, Sophie, who would stay with her for the night in case of concussion.

Nina had had multiple crashes in her career, as most drivers did. She'd adhered to her safety protocols and kept her cool, much to the compliments of the team, but still…knowing she'd been so close to her first podium finish hurt more than any amount of bruising or damaged pride. She knew that she didn't have a concussion, but still she was happy for Sophie's company on the long walk out past the roaring crowds and into a car.

She had foolishly expected Tristan to rush to her side, considering he'd been right above the crash site and had likely had a full view of the entire incident. But he hadn't appeared in the medical bay, nor had he shown up to check on her in her motorhome with the rest of the management team. She'd been half tempted to text him, to chastise him for jeopardising the legitimacy of their precious ruse. What kind of fiancé didn't rush to his lover's side when she'd been injured?

Her needy thoughts had felt silly and pathetic, and she'd angrily shrugged them off, instead opting for the far more mature option of ordering multiple fried foods and desserts to her hotel room, much to the eye-rolling of her beleaguered trainer.

'I'm just saying there are healthier forms of ice cream on the market now,' Sophie grumbled as they stepped out of the car service and into the foyer of the team hotel.

'I don't want healthy, I want sugar,' Nina gritted, laying a gentle punch on her long-time friend's elbow. 'If you're nice to me I might even share.'

'Looks like someone else might have a different idea,' Sophie said cryptically. 'Like maybe a little Argentine tango for two?'

'Tango is always for two, that's a given.' Nina stopped speaking as she caught sight of the *someone else* Sophie had just referenced.

Tristan strode across the hotel foyer, directly towards her. When she'd briefly imagined him rushing to her side while the medic had checked out her bruises, she'd envisioned a little more swoon and romance, but instead he came to a stop in front of her, a scowl transforming his usually flirty features.

'The doctors cleared you?' he asked, mouth tight with tension.

'I'm completely fine. I just need to go to bed.'

'We were supposed to attend the big party, but I offered to stay with her in case of concussion,' Sophie said awkwardly, looking from Tristan's furious face to Nina's impassive one with rampant curiosity.

'There's no need for you to miss the event. Nina will be staying with me.'

'I most certainly will not be—'

'Nina,' he gritted, turning a forced smile to Sophie. 'Thank you for getting her back safely. Enjoy the party.'

To her horror, he simply grabbed her by the elbow and directed her towards the private elevator that led to the penthouse suite, leaving Sophie waggling her eyebrows gleefully in their wake.

'Stop manhandling me. You're walking way too fast.'

He paused, looking down at her with a stricken expression before returning to a slightly more gentle form of manhandling, straight into the lift.

'This elevator only goes to the penthouse. Your things have already been delivered to my bedroom,' he stated, punching the only button on the dial and exhaling a long breath as the elevator stuttered and then began to move smoothly upwards. 'Don't fight me on this. I'm already only just about holding it together as it is.'

'I'm sorry if you had plans to socialise and be photographed this evening, but I don't see how my injury has to change any of that.'

Midnight blue eyes narrowed upon her. 'You think I'm bothered about us missing a photo call right now?'

'Aren't you? Your top priority is your reputation, that's what this little fake engagement ruse is all about after all.'

'That was before…' He paused, eyes closed and a pained expression on his face. For a moment she wondered if he was about to pounce, as he had that night in Milan when she'd dared him to. But all too quickly, the elevator doors slid open to reveal a long hall and two security guards. Tristan greeted the men by name, guiding her down the ornate hallway to a set of tall double doors.

The grand royal suite inside was as lavish and needlessly large as one would expect. It was modern and airy, but still held an air of history, as though it had been recently vacated by the kings and queens it had been named for. Priceless gold-framed artworks hung on every wall, and the ceilings were high and ornate with tiny cherubs carved into the moulding.

'My own room was perfectly fine,' she couldn't resist griping as she followed along behind him through the cavernous hallway. 'You could fit the entire team up here and still have space for a ball.'

'I'll get right on that, once I've made sure you haven't passed out from your injuries.'

'I'm fine.' Tiredness washed over her and for once she didn't feel like fighting him. 'You don't have to watch me, but I suppose that's what my fiancé would do.'

'I don't care what I should do right now. Not when I've just watched you smack into a metal wall at almost three hundred kilometres an hour.'

'It wasn't that fast. I had just decelerated from a turn, remember.'

He narrowed his eyes wildly upon her once more, his deft hands pausing inside the first-aid bag he'd produced.

'I've already been checked and cleared by the medical team, Tristan, no cuts and no visible wounds of any kind, other than minor bruising.'

'I know. I spoke to them over the phone and had a second opinion phoned in by my physician in Paris.'

'You did?'

'Yes. I did.' He met her eyes, his mouth opening for a second as though he might add to that but, instead, he just went back to gathering more medicines and an ice pack from the case.

He guided her into the massive master bedroom, insisting that was where she would sleep tonight. Growing more groggy and tired by the minute, Nina didn't argue when he kneeled down to remove her running shoes and helped her peel off the cotton yoga pants and baggy T-shirt she had hastily changed into after the medical team had finished scanning her entire body for internal bleeding and fractures. As calm and cool as she pretended to be, hitting the wall at such high speed was not a minor thing.

In fact, it was the one incident she had managed to avoid her entire career thus far, having only heard anecdotal accounts from other drivers about the shocking pressure of the gravitational forces that came with travelling at exceptionally high speeds. If you put a solid metal barrier in front of that speed unexpectedly, well... She had been incredibly lucky today.

Maybe that sense of relief was why she didn't stop Tristan from fussing over her pillows as she took the pain relief medication he'd laid out. He guided her back against the pillows he'd adjusted but then surprised her by lying down next to her on the bed.

'Get comfortable here, because you are not leaving this bed.'

Nina rolled over to her side so that she could look at him, wincing when even that hurt. 'Don't threaten me with a good time, Falco. Your three-day wait is up— am I finally about to get the full playboy experience?'

He turned to face her, and for the first time she realised that he had removed his suit jacket and tie. She took in the bared skin on show, the strong column of his throat and the top of his tanned chest beneath. When she looked up to see his eyes had darkened upon her, she swallowed audibly.

Tristan made a low tutting sound, reaching out to place the back of his hand against her now flushed cheek. 'Utterly insatiable...even with a possible mild concussion. Is that truly what you're thinking about right now?'

'You made me promise you, after all,' she whispered, shivering as his knuckles trailed down to skate along the side of her neck and bare shoulder.

'Even I have my limits when it comes to focusing on certain situations.' His brows furrowed, his hand sweeping down the outside of her arm where light bruising was already beginning to appear.

'How can someone be so fearless and strong, and still be so utterly breakable?'

She wasn't sure if he had intended to speak those words aloud, and the sudden strain in his voice hit her squarely in the chest. She realised then that his snappy, irritated caretaking was not exasperation as she had assumed, but possibly...worry? For her?

'So you've skipped out on your big event to tuck me into bed?' she asked quietly.

'You need to rest. And I'm here to make sure that you actually do that.'

'You've waylaid all my self-destructive plans for the night, I assure you. Sophie is likely very relieved. I told her I planned to order every dessert on the menu and then eat every single one while watching as many romantic comedies as I can find. She hates romance almost as much as she hates refined sugar.'

'But you don't?'

'Romcoms have always been my go-to for when I'm overwhelmed. They're like medicine, they help me calm down and...regulate.' She used the last word deliberately, gauging his reaction to the rather clinical term. She'd often wondered if her personal collection of unique strengths, differences and challenges were perhaps symptoms of something more. Something that her parents hadn't noticed or hadn't known to look for. But after seeing Astrid on the yacht, she'd done a little research and it turned out she ticked quite a number of boxes.

Tristan frowned. 'I can see how that would help. I usually prefer action-adventure-type films, but my mother and I would watch all the classic romantic comedies together to learn English. I had quite an interesting vocabulary for a number of years.'

'You're close with your mother,' she said tiredly, her eyelids drooping as she fought off sleep. 'I have no idea what that must be like. That kind of...easy love. I didn't have that with mine. We're too different, I think.'

'It's not always easy,' he said honestly. 'Back then it was even easier, when we had my uncle to play referee between us. But yes, we were always close.'

She didn't miss the furrow in his brows at the mention of his uncle, nor the way he quickly got up off the bed and set about ordering them both a copious amount of dessert from room service. She focused on staying awake as long as she could, but eventually not even the sugar or her favourite romcom could do the job.

She slid into a dream-filled sleep where Tristan watched over her like a guardian angel, his strong hands gently petting her hair while he whispered passionate words in his native tongue. Dream Tristan smelled just as divine as the real-life version and she allowed herself to burrow her face into his skin, breathing him in with a groan of approval. How easy this would be to get used to, she mused as she crawled up higher against his solid male chest and felt his low rumble of amusement as her lips clumsily pressed against his.

'You make me wish this were real,' she murmured, half on a sigh. 'Making me...want you.'

'I'm right here, *mi querida*,' her dream lover whispered against her mouth. 'I'm yours.'

Tristan opened his eyes to the sight of sunlight streaming in through the windows and Nina fast asleep in his arms. He'd managed to sleep the whole night through somehow, despite the little minx's determination to press every inch of her lithe body against his. Testing his muscles, he was pretty sure he hadn't moved once through the night. A quick look at his watch showed it was just dawn.

He had done his best to keep Nina awake and talking for as long as possible until her eyes had begun to droop and she had become completely unintelligible. Once he was sure that her sleep was safe and not one born of deep concussion, his own body had eventually begun to relax. That was, until she'd begun mumbling and moaning in her sleep, seemingly determined to have her way with him. Her clumsy kiss and sleep-induced longing had kept him awake far longer than he'd like to admit as he pondered his own tangle of emotions. Adrenaline really was the best form of sleeping tablet and he'd eventually fallen asleep with her nestled safely in his arms.

But now that he was awake, the anxiety from the day before came back in full force. After Nina had hit the wall and everyone had gone into a panic, Tristan's anxiety had taken over and he found himself needing to retreat so as not to do something reckless. He never knew when his panic would impede his day-to-day life. It had become such an immovable part of him over the past decade since the accident that had ended his uncle's life prematurely. His beloved uncle, who had been such an important father figure to him, as he'd never known his own. A man who'd fallen apart after the death of his wife, a wonderful woman Tristan had also loved dearly. He'd never been able to reach his uncle through the years of deep grief that had followed. His disengagement with life meant he should never have been flying the plane he'd crashed, killing himself but thankfully not Tristan, the only passenger on board. He closed his eyes, feeling the familiar tension in his chest rising as his ears imagined the sound of screaming jets and rushing air.

His post-traumatic stress disorder was something he managed, but not something he would ever be free of. The aeroplane accident would always be a part of him, even if it had taken him a number of painful years to accept that. Still, old wounds flared up hard and he was using every one of the tools and strategies he'd ever learned to keep himself in check.

Carefully, he disentangled his arm from beneath Nina's head and slid backwards until he could quietly slip out of bed. He still wore his clothing from the day before minus his shoes and coat, but the collar of his shirt felt too tight and he resisted the urge to rip it off himself in one move.

He hardly remembered getting on the phone and bellowing at his own private doctor in Paris for a second opinion on Nina's injuries. The small number of executives who had followed him from the guest spectators' suite had looked upon him with shock and possible fear, he'd likely seemed so unhinged. It was a part of himself he'd worked hard to keep under wraps, so uncomfortable he was with the unpredictability of his own reactions once he'd been triggered. And so Tristan had been forced to leave the paddock to calm down, once he knew that Nina would be following him quickly enough.

Making his way through to the living room area of his suite, he quietly called through to the concierge and ordered coffee and breakfast to be sent up shortly. Nina would need to wake in order to take her medication and she couldn't do that on an empty stomach. The domesticity of that thought made him pause but strangely, for once, it didn't make him want to scream and run. He wanted to care for Nina in a way that he had never felt the urge to care for anyone before. It was a feeling that he couldn't quite explain away with simple sexual attraction.

Sure, he very much wanted to bed her at his earliest convenience, but he also wanted to make sure that she was eating enough and that she wasn't working too damned hard. She was too independent for her own good, and was always thinking of the team and her charity, never about herself.

She could have *died* yesterday.

And yet all she'd been worried about once she'd emerged from that car was missing out on the damned podium place. It had made him feel so furious and helpless—two emotions he greatly disliked feeling. Well, he'd taken control of himself now and he'd decided she was going to be forced to rest and to prioritise herself for once. Even if she fought him tooth and nail the entire time—in fact, he hoped she would. He loved it when she fought him.

This tangle of thoughts held him frozen in place on the balcony as he stared out at the sun rising above the city of Barcelona. He almost didn't hear the terrace door sliding open behind him until Nina appeared by his side, wrapped in a fluffy white robe.

'I wasn't going to wake you until breakfast arrived,' he said, gesturing for her to take a seat alongside him.

'It's gorgeous.' She sighed, her eyes glued to the sky putting on a show as the dawn broke fully. 'It's the most stunning thing I've ever seen.'

'It really is,' Tristan murmured in agreement, his eyes not leaving her face. She turned to look at him, a slight blush creeping to her cheeks.

'How's the pain?' he asked, scanning her face for traces of discomfort.

'I feel rather how one would expect to after slamming into an immovable object at high speed.'

Tristan winced, turning back to look out at the domes of the roofs in an effort to distract himself from the overwhelming urge to demand she never set foot in a race car again.

'Sorry, Tristan, I'm honestly fine. I've never hit the wall before, not that hard anyway. But we are trained to encounter all emergencies, so I knew what to do to keep myself safe. The cars are safe, our apparatus is safe… I'm safe too.'

'Luckily,' Tristan growled. 'This time.'

Her lips pursed tight. 'Luck does have a part to play in it. But I'd also like to think that my skill and my commitment to using the correct techniques at all times are also in my favour. For the number of races I've started, I've got an exceptionally low damage record.'

'I'm not saying that you're not skilled, Nina. You didn't cause that incident yesterday. I've already asked the team principal to issue a protest to the stewards to get that bastard suspended.'

'You did what?' She gasped, wincing a little at the pain in her shoulder as she turned to face him.

'We all saw how he attacked you, recklessly trying to move ahead when he didn't have the room. He will be severely penalised, if I have my way. He's lucky if that's all he gets away with. I just don't understand how you can get back in the driver's seat after an event like that.'

'Because it's my *job*, Tristan.' She tilted her chin up defiantly. 'I just as easily could have miscalculated during an overtaking manoeuvre and caused *them* to hydroplane. Would you seek to have me suspended from the sport if that were the case?'

He remained silent, holding his tongue at what he wished to say. What he wished to demand. If their engagement were real and they'd been planning to intertwine their lives, perhaps he might have spoken those thoughts aloud, but it wasn't his place. Maybe it wasn't his place either way. It *was* her job, after all.

But no job was worth more than one's life. His uncle had learned that the hard way.

They were interrupted by the sound of a knock at the door and the next while was a pleasant distraction of a delicious breakfast, which they both practically inhaled, neither of them having eaten since early the evening before. Once they were pleasantly full and their plates had been cleared away, Nina stood and announced that she was going to get ready.

'Get ready for what, exactly?'

She looked at him, hands on her hips. 'I appreciate you taking care of me last night, Tristan, but we both have separate plans. You need to be back in Paris today and I have to pack for the photo shoot. And I'd like to get a workout in before I leave.'

'First of all, you are on bed rest. And secondly, I will not be going to Paris. I'll be escorting you to the Falco estate.'

'You will? Does that mean that you've decided to do the photo shoot?'

'No,' he growled. 'It means that I will be coming with you, and I will oversee the photo shoot to make sure that it goes according to my specifications.'

'I rather feel like you are babysitting me.' She narrowed her eyes at him. 'But okay, then.'

'That's it?' He narrowed his own suspiciously. 'No five-minute sermon about how you don't need to be babysat by me and how I'm stifling your independence by ordering you around?'

She smiled. She actually smiled at his outrage, the little brat.

'No argument. I'll go back and then we can leave.' She sauntered over to the bathroom, pausing for a split second at the doorway. 'You know, I think I kind of like it when you order me around.'

She smirked, disappearing into the bathroom and leaving him to groan into his own hands with the effort of not following her.

After being firmly denied her suggestion of a gentle swim before they left, Nina remained quiet and on edge for most of their journey as they travelled north along the Spanish coast. Resisting the urge to ask the hundred burning questions that entered her mind, she almost picked through the skin on the beds of her nails as they began to move further and further away from the city.

Going without heavy exercise for two days straight might not be much to most people, but, as someone used to a certain amount of challenging physical activity per day, the lack of release was rapidly sending her anxiety levels through the roof.

Sophie had sent her a number of probing texts to see if she was doing okay, her trainer likely remembering how easily Nina had slid into burnout after her neck injury a couple of years ago. The long period of bed rest and slow torturous rehabilitation had been painful on so much more than just her injured body. She had always known that she didn't cope well with slowing down, but now, looking at her difficulties through a new lens, she realised that it was possible her neurodivergent brain actually *needed* to keep busy. That maybe it was okay that she relied so heavily on having measurable goals to focus on and tasks to hit in order to feel any semblance of balance. Perhaps there was no need to feel so ashamed of how rigidly she clung to her schedule. Much like the temperamental vehicles she drove, if she stopped too suddenly, she risked fully losing control.

'Still cranky?' Tristan asked, breaking her out of her own thought spiral.

For once she was actually grateful for the distraction. 'Just trying to ascertain if you always drive at this speed, or if you're crawling along in the slow lane just to irritate me.'

He smirked, his hands drumming a beat on the wheel as he slowed even further. 'Maybe I like to enjoy the scenery when I travel. Live in the moment.'

'Well, you'll have a lot of scenery to enjoy, seeing as we likely won't arrive until tomorrow.' She pressed the button on the dash to try and find some music to distract herself, only to be met with her least favourite big summer dance tune. She winced, turning the volume back down.

'My radio, my rules,' he scolded, turning the dial back up and singing along with the overdramatic tune. He sang well, annoyingly well. Of course he had been blessed with the voice of a fallen angel as well as having the looks of one. Still, she had to turn her head to watch as he bellowed the fast-paced Spanish lyrics, describing the famous singer's scorn after her lover had strayed. He knew every single word. She thought of how intensely he'd reacted after her accident.

Was it possible that he actually wasn't quite the paragon of calm that he pretended to be? This man sang the song with a quiet passion that made her skin prickle and her heart throb. He *felt* the lyrics. Too soon, the song came to an end and she felt as if she'd just witnessed yet another tiny glimpse beneath the mask of Tristan Falco. Something even wilder and more intense than the devil-may-care playboy he presented to the world.

The Falco estate was as grand and exaggerated as she expected it to be, with a sweeping tree-lined drive that seemed to go on for miles before the actual house came into view—well, Tristan had referred to it as a house but as they grew closer, she could hardly believe her eyes.

'Is that a freaking castle?' she asked.

'The main house dates back to the seventeenth century, yes.' Tristan smiled. 'My uncle had a flair for the dramatic, and once he saw this place nothing else would do.'

Nina had grown up in luxury and was no stranger

to the opulent grand estates of wealthy families, but the Falco estate was nothing like she had ever seen before. After parking in the middle of a grand courtyard, complete with legitimate antique marble statues and a manicured garden that would make a king weep, Tristan greeted the couple who managed the estate year-round and linked his arm through Nina's as they were given a grand tour.

He introduced her as his fiancée, of course, which the housekeeper and her husband acknowledged with delight, asking if the wedding was to be held upon the estate. Without missing a beat, Tristan mentioned that his mother would likely insist it took place in Buenos Aires. It was just part of their ruse, she reminded herself. But still, hearing him mention their non-existent wedding plans shifted something in her stomach.

Her sense of awe quickly overrode her unease at their deception as she was guided through the most stunningly preserved historic estate she had ever seen. She was given the full history by the very animated groundskeeper, his wife interrupting every now and then to correct him if he got the dates wrong. The majestic manor house was located in the most exclusive area of Barcelona's north coast, less than an hour from the city centre. Surrounded by beautiful garden and lush forests, it was gloriously private with breathtaking views of the Mediterranean Sea. They were shown around more than ten spacious suites inside, then guided outside where there were a large ballroom and chapel hidden in some lush forest, as well as a long swimming pool and a handful of smaller villas.

The main building was comprised of several out-buildings that formed a fortified enclosure. It had been reformed over time while preserving and enhancing the architectural wealth of the original stone features. Its charm lay in the perfect fusion of its historical charac-ter with the more modern touches that added comfort and luxury.

Tristan seemed on friendly terms with the staff, which surprised her considering she had read he'd grown up mostly in Buenos Aires with his mother, with the excep-tion of his teenage years when he'd attended a boarding school somewhere in Europe. She knew so little about him, she realised.

The couple didn't live on the estate, she learned, they instead ran a small restaurant in the nearby town along with their grown-up children. They invited them to come for dinner that evening, before bidding them farewell and leaving them alone.

'So this place just sits here empty, year-round?'

'My mother has held a few events here over the years but, yes, since my uncle's passing, no one has lived here. This was his home and he commuted to the Falco head-quarters every day. He even converted one of the villas on the property into a home for me. He loved it here. He had horses and dreamed of running his own personal tours for the public, free of charge, when he retired.'

But when they reached the end of the stables where a large building bridged off in a long rectangle, Tristan paused. Nina looked up, not missing the shutters that seemed to instantly come down, hardening his hand-some features.

'His garage,' he said, reaching into his pocket to extract a key and placing it in her palm. 'He had a few cars, so, while we're here, you may as well select which model you would like to use for tomorrow.'

'You don't want to choose it with me?' she asked, confused.

He shook his head, already turning away. 'I need to do a walk around of the few setting locations while there is still light. The magazine's team will be here early in the morning; it will save us time if they know where to set up.'

She nodded, watching him stride across the lawn. The doors to the garage were automatic and slid upwards with ease once she turned the key. She had only a few seconds of squinting into the darkness before lights flickered on overhead one by one, until the entire cavernous space was lit, revealing much more than the small collection of cars Tristan had intimated was in there.

Nina's heart pumped in her chest as she began to walk along the rows, not quite knowing where to look first as she was met with what had to be around fifty perfectly preserved classic cars. Each one of them bearing her family's symbol on their bonnet.

'My God,' she whispered, spotting a particular model given pride of place on a raised podium at the end of the hall. For a moment she contemplated dropping to her knees, feeling as though she had entered a hallowed space of some sort. She supposed, to people who worshipped cars, it didn't really get much better than this.

The first edition Roux Motors coupe was one she had

never actually seen in person, as only five had ever been built. Two had met their fate in fiery crashes in various parts of the globe and the other two that she knew of had been sold to collectors' museums in Asia. This particular car had passed through a number of nameless private owners, as far as she knew. It had been the car used in a very famous film with an equally famous lead actor playing the role of a spy.

She ran her fingertips along the buttery soft column of the steering wheel, noting the fresh smell of leather polish and the lack of dust upon the bonnet. If this garage had been left unattended for as long as Tristan had said, that meant he was employing someone to keep them valeted. A person would only do that if they also cared about the vehicles within. No harm would come from letting a collection like this gather a little dust. But she could tell by the gleam on each of the cars, and the scent of pine in the air, that this collection was beloved. Polished and ready for display, as though the previous owner had never left.

The way Tristan had spoken of his uncle, the fact that he had been given his own home on the property... It spoke of a very close bond between the two men. Tristan had even said he'd been more like a father to him. And to think that Tristan had almost lost his life in the same aeroplane accident that had killed someone so important to him... It was more than she could bear thinking of.

When she finally tracked him down, he stood in the courtyard with an impressively large camera in his hands as he surveyed a particularly ragged-looking fallen tree trunk in the woodland that bordered the property.

'You see one you liked?' he asked, the sound of the camera shutter flicking periodically as he changed view and moved back and forth a few steps.

'I feel like I just went to church.' She came to a stop by his side, peering over his shoulder to take in the image he'd captured of a butterfly landing on one of the craggy branches.

'I thought you'd feel that way. Half of all the Roux Motors' models ever made are in there, if not more,' Tristan murmured, clearing his throat as he continued to glower down at the fallen tree. 'He was only missing four that he wanted, before he…well, before. When the news broke that your father was selling his collection, he was one of the first to bid.'

She pursed her lips, remembering that chaotic time when her father's scandalous gambling debts and impending bankruptcy had been all over the news. The Falco plane crash had happened that same week. In another universe, how might it have gone if instead of Alain taking the helm, Tristan's uncle had bought them out and preserved Roux Motors with all of the passion she'd felt in that garage?

'He used to joke that he would name the first car he produced the Dulce Diablo after my mother. My mother always teased him for his collection and how much time he spent there, leaving all the party invitations to her. But he was obsessed.'

'I would have got along quite well with him, I'd imagine,' Nina mused, sitting down upon the thick trunk of the fallen tree. 'We'd have shared a bond in our fascination over cars and engines…and you.'

'You're fascinated with me, hmm?' Tristan asked, holding the camera up to his eye again and flicking the shutter a few times.

'I am. Hopelessly so.' Nina felt the air shift around them from his difficult past, the sunlight dappling her skin as if to remind her that she was in fact here right now. Living in the moment, as he'd said before. He was so tense, so burdened by the memory of being here in this place. Maybe she could help him with that, give him some new, happier memories. Making the decision to be brave, she slid down one strap of her dress.

CHAPTER EIGHT

BEING BACK IN the home where he had shared so many happy memories with his uncle and aunt before they'd both died had already put Tristan on edge for most of the day. But that was nothing compared to the torture of watching Nina slide down the straps of her summer dress. The loose cotton material easily skimmed over her toned curves, before sliding down to pool around her ankles, leaving her in skimpy underwear.

'Shoes on or off?' she asked meekly, kicking the dress to one side and leaning back against the tree trunk.

'Shoes?'

She smiled, gesturing down to the trainers she still wore. 'The magazine wants me to be in swimwear tomorrow, so I feel like these should come off too, no?'

The simple *yes* that escaped his lips was little more than a croak, and he cleared his throat, frowning down at the display of his camera to click a few random buttons. He was doing absolutely nothing productive of course; with his automatic high-grade apparatus a lot of it was done automatically.

'Is that completely necessary?' she asked, raising an eyebrow.

He grunted a reply, getting down into a crouch in the grass. He narrowed his eyes on her, suddenly realising what kind of game his little cat was playing. He'd denied her request last night, not willing to risk her injuries might be more serious than either of them had assumed. But now, apart from a little light bruising here and there, she was most certainly fighting fit and determined to break down his chivalrous control in whatever way she could.

'Lean back and arch your neck,' he growled, satisfied, when she looked up at him with surprise.

'Like this?' She leaned back in the way he'd directed, attentive and serene as he instructed her to place her body this way and that, then to move one ankle over the other.

'Soften your lower lip, *querida*,' he breathed. 'Yes, that's it. Now…look directly at me. Don't look away until I tell you.'

'Or else, what?' She narrowed that onyx gaze on him.

'Perhaps I'll decide that this photo shoot needs even less clothing.' Through the lens of the camera, he zoomed in, seeing the very moment that her pupils dilated and her nostrils flared.

Little minx. He'd bet she was imagining it right now, him ordering her to strip off her underwear, exposing her bared flesh to him and his camera. They were all alone out here after all… He could easily follow through on his threat. The idea of it made his blood thrum in his ears and he almost entirely lost focus on his act of taking photos completely. Nina wasn't doing too much better as she fixed her lust-hazed eyes on him, her arms beginning to shake with the effort of leaning back on the rough surface of the tree trunk.

'Breathe, Nina,' he murmured, moving a few steps closer and continuing to click, at speed. He caught the moment her eyes turned sultry, and the blush that had been kissing only her cheeks swept down to cover her chest.

'You're a natural at this…so beautiful.' He ignored the tightening of his raging erection, focusing on her, on nothing but her as she obeyed his instructions. 'Good, Nina. So good.'

She practically blossomed under his praise, her nipples tightening into little peaks beneath her bra as she thrust her breasts forward and spread her legs wide of her own accord. She posed herself this way and that, loosening up under his gaze.

He had never actually done a posed photo shoot with a model this way. He'd always preferred to find his subjects in real life, unaware. Catching the little moments of honesty. But this, whatever they were doing here, felt like a perfect meeting of the two styles. A mixture of instruction and honesty that made his skin feel too tight and his heart beat too loud in his ears. He had held himself in check with this woman for weeks on end, determined to deny his own pleasure. While it seemed she had slowly realised that there was one thing she wanted from their deal, the one thing that he had told her he could not, should not, give her.

Dropping the camera down to his side, he replaced the mechanical gaze upon her with his own and saw her beautiful features soften even more. She didn't move out of her pose, the one he'd put her in. Like the cat he'd compared her to, she lay in wait. Those onyx eyes didn't leave his as he took one step closer followed by another and another until he had her pressed up against his chest. His lips found hers as if he were a magnet and she his true North, and he plundered and possessed every inch of her mouth before coming up for air.

'You drive me wild,' he rasped, fisting his hands in her hair to keep her in place or to keep himself tethered perhaps. He felt out of control, more out of control than he'd ever been, but he welcomed it. He welcomed the adventure that was Nina… The passion and the infuriating fire that she had brought back into his life replacing the numbness of mediocrity and boredom. It would reappear all too soon once they went their separate ways again.

Sliding his hands down along her sides, he allowed himself to stop overthinking everything and simply feel. The sensation of her silky-smooth skin under his fingertips was heaven, as was the delicate way she rocked her pelvis against his erection. Needy moans escaped her lips as she peppered his throat with hungry kisses.

'I'm supposed to be the one seducing you,' he growled.

'Says who?' She looked up at him through long sooty lashes, a sensual smile on her lips.

'You really liked it when I ordered you around.'

A fresh blush crept up her cheeks, and she tilted her head down bashfully.

He put one finger under her chin, encouraging her to look back up at him. 'Those photos are all yours, by the way. To keep or delete as you wish. I don't need a photograph for what's already burned in my memory, *querida*. But I do need to get you to a bed fairly soon.'

'A bed...*yes*.' She whispered the words in between moans and delicious whimpers as he bent his head to busy himself with one taut nipple through the thin material of her bra. Forcing himself to move, he stood back up, took her by the hand and led her towards his villa.

The journey from their little interlude was a complete blur and Nina soon felt her frantically aroused body pushed back onto Tristan's huge four-poster bed, giggling wildly as his equally frantic form spread over her.

He murmured pretty words against her mouth, his hands clumsily working to undo his belt. The room was dimly lit with the curtains drawn, but she could just about make out his muscular form as he straightened to pull off his T-shirt and shuck off his jeans. He was upon her again in an instant, his hot skin sliding against her own in the most blissful sensation. Her entire body felt like a livewire that had been activated. She wanted him everywhere.

'I'm afraid this first time might not last very long.' Gently, he spread her thighs wide and Nina gasped at the sensation of him *right there*.

'I don't want to crush you...you're sure your injuries aren't—'

'Tristan. I'm fine. But if you stop right now, I swear...'

He laughed, lying on his side to pull her against his chest as he ripped open a foil packet and slid protection over his length with impressive speed. With one hand, he pulled her thigh up so that her body half straddled him.

She'd done some research to feel more prepared but this position was not one she'd ever seen in a movie or read about in a book. It felt impossibly intimate with his eyes on hers and almost every inch of their skin touching. His erection was hot and heavy against her entrance as his finger traced a slow circle right where she needed it.

'*Please,*' she begged, grinding herself against him. 'Oh, my God.'

'Slow…slow down, *por el amor de Dios*, or I swear I won't last more than five seconds.'

'You said you never lose control.'

'I say a lot of foolish things around you.' He caught her mouth in another punishing kiss as he pressed forward, sliding the very tip of himself inside her. The slight stretch felt uncomfortable but not overly so and with his lips devouring hers so passionately she quickly forgot to worry about pain, eager for more. With his eyes on hers there was nowhere to hide, but she didn't feel self-conscious, she felt beautiful. She felt desirable and sexy and right. More right than she'd ever felt, even behind the wheel.

The combination of him at her entrance and against her clitoris was magic and she quickly felt her legs begin to tremble with the onset of release. He didn't speed up, nor did he look away or react as she whispered a series of curses and prayers in French. He was right there with her, holding her with his quiet strength as he ruthlessly worked her body in a perfect rhythm until she broke apart.

Her orgasm was a slow earthquake that swept up from her toes to her chin, wiping out every coherent thought she had and turning her into a shaking mass of limbs against his chest. She was vaguely aware of his lips pressing tenderly against her brow and of the fact that he hadn't seemed to experience the same release as she had.

'That was…perfect,' she whispered, unable to stop the smile that spread up to her cheeks.

'Perfect,' he murmured. 'I need to hear you come again before I do, but I need to be fully inside you.'

'That wasn't…fully inside?' she whispered, shaking herself out of the haze of her post-orgasmic bubble.

He let out a husky laugh, already bracing himself over her and spreading her thighs wide. 'My ego needs no further stroking, *mi cielo*, I'm already on the edge as it is.'

Nina tensed up, trying to find the right words to tell him that *fully inside* might not be an option just yet, but all thoughts left her as he gently slid his thumb over her still-sensitive core in a slow firm circle. All thoughts subsided, replaced by a heady rush of sensation and heat that made her groan aloud. This man was going to overdose her with orgasms before the night was through, she was sure of it. She looked up at him, pleasure drunk, and was struck anew at how handsome he was. Seized with a sense of bravery, she told him as much in a breathless voice that sounded nothing like her own.

He smiled. The next thing she was aware of was him pressing his length into her with one smooth thrust.

The pain was so sharp, so sudden that Nina whimpered, a guttural sound escaping her throat as she braced both hands against his powerful chest with the urge to push him away. Tristan immediately froze, brows furrowed as he settled himself and his massive member right where it was apparently attempting to split her apart.

'You…you're too tight, *belleza*,' he gritted, a slow breath hissing through his teeth as he held himself frozen in place.

'You're too large,' she countered. 'Oh…my God.'

'Not that large.' He shook his head slightly, a horrified expression transforming his face. 'Nina, are you…? Is this…?'

'My first time, yes,' she finished for him. 'I'm okay, it's already feeling better. Don't stop.'

A low series of curses followed, his brow dropping to press against the junction of her neck and shoulders. *'Dios… Nina.'*

She placed her hands on either side of his face, lifting him until his tortured gaze met hers. 'I'm fine now. Don't you dare stop.'

His expression hardened, a vein popping in his temple as he visibly wrestled with emotions she couldn't quite name but would hazard a guess about. She'd thought he'd understood her lack of experience, but she should have made it crystal-clear to him. But even so, she would not apologise for how tonight had gone. Nor would she change any of it. Unless he walked away right now— *that* she would not recover from too easily.

He didn't seem fully deterred by her revelation, not judging by how his length still pressed hot and hard inside her. Plus, it didn't seem to hurt quite so much now that they'd taken a small breather. Curious, she experimented, tightening her inner muscles around him with a slow squeeze. Tristan's eyes drifted closed so she did it again, this time eliciting a low growl from his lips.

'You're trying to kill me.' He groaned. 'You needed me to be much more gentle with you. I shouldn't have—'

'I don't *want* gentle, Tristan.' She moved again, a swift tilt of her hips to grind up against him. She was clumsy and unpractised but not entirely without skill, it seemed, as his eyes opened again and he finally, finally began to move once more. Slowly at first, but his restraint quickly faltered as his breathing grew more ragged. She felt the power in every thrust, as though both of them were fighting against one another but somehow moving perfectly in time. Like a dance. As though every other interaction they'd had had been building towards this.

Was this what their fighting had been about? Perhaps she had never hated him at all.

There was no other word for how it felt to have him taking her this way other than complete possession and it was over far too soon. She gasped and climaxed for the second time and, with a loud roar, Tristan shuddered against her and collapsed, his breath fanning against her cheek for a second before he gently withdrew. He lay on his back alongside her and they stayed like that for a long moment, their chests rising and falling in tandem.

After a long silence, Nina felt him move away. A click of the bathroom light followed and the running of water. He returned moments later, gently guiding her so he could use a warm compress to cleanse between her legs. When he pulled the towel away, a small amount of blood stained the white cotton. Squinting in the low light, she saw the furrow between his brows and the tension in his shoulders. She wanted to soothe him, to reassure him that tonight had been perfect. She wanted to apologise for being too shy to tell him that she hadn't technically had sex before, but that she was glad he'd been her first. She wanted him to kiss her again and tell her that he was glad too.

'Sleep.' He spoke softly, but made no move to join her again in the bed.

Nina watched as he pulled on a robe and walked to the high balcony windows that overlooked the coastline, his broad silhouette framed in the light of the moon. She fought off the sleep that threatened to claim her. It wasn't meant to feel this way, getting her wish. She was supposed to feel empowered and satisfied, having very thoroughly got the Falco experience.

He'd been everything she'd fantasised about and more, but a whole new ache had been opened up within her, entirely unrelated to the dull throbbing between her legs. She realised with alarm that the ache had now settled in her chest, bringing with it a longing for the man who seemed so intent on holding her at a distance while he possessed her every waking thought.

She wanted much more than to be just another woman who'd lost herself in his bed. She wanted him to lose himself with her. To need more of her, just as she seemed unable to stop needing more of him. All these thoughts seemed so urgent as he turned around, walking back over to the bedside to quietly ask if she was okay. But that dreamy haze still pulled at her mind and all she managed was a husky 'thank you' before she fell into a deep, satisfied sleep.

CHAPTER NINE

NINA'S SLEEPY THANK YOU rang in Tristan's ears long after she'd dozed off and left him alone with his thoughts. She'd been a virgin. A virgin in his bed and he'd had no idea. He'd trusted the chemistry between them, been blinded by his own lust so much that he'd missed all of the signs. Now he could see that, while she might not have specifically referred to herself in such terms, she'd tried to let him know that she wasn't experienced.

Still, he was furious with himself.

The image of her face wincing with pain after he thrust inside her would be burned into his memory for ever. He'd taken her without any finesse, so eager he'd been to possess her. He'd hurt her...

Hour after hour in the dark, he wrestled with his unsettling thoughts until he gave up and slid back into bed alongside her. Staring into her sleeping face, he realised why he was so angry with himself for not seeing the signs of her inexperience. It wasn't about his ego or his reputation in the bedroom. When he was with Nina, none of that mattered. It was because he cared. She was rapidly beginning to matter to him in a way he couldn't look at too closely. It made his chest feel tight, his throat dry and painful as he reached out to run his knuckles over the silky skin of her bare shoulder.

The idea that she'd seen tonight as a temporary experiment of sorts did nothing to ease his temper. He'd have to set her to rights on *that* tomorrow. Once he'd cooled off. Maybe even once they'd made love again and he'd shown her exactly how it should have been the first time and how he planned for it to be every time after that for the foreseeable future if he got his way.

With that thought settling with some satisfaction inside his chest, he pulled her sleeping form against his chest and let her delicious scent carry him off into a deep sleep.

Nina didn't know what a person was expected to feel or say the morning after having sex with a fake fiancé, but after Tristan's silence the night before she didn't plan on sticking around until he woke up to find out.

The morning sun was pleasant and warm on her face as she took a long walk through the tree-lined woods that surrounded the castle grounds, letting the effect of gentle exercise in nature smooth out some of the knots that had taken up residence in her muscles. Sex was a more strenuous workout than she'd anticipated, she thought with a small smile as she set about grabbing some coffee and fruit from the long buffet table that the housekeeper had set up for the crew.

She briefly greeted the few who had arrived early to set up the shoots for the day, then decided it was best to keep out of the way until someone told her otherwise. Still, her nerves tightened and she felt more twitchy and uncomfortable with every second she tried to remain calmly seated on the patio that overlooked the pool. Dark sunglasses shielded her sensitive eyes from view at least, so she whiled away some time with a game on her phone until the sound of heavy footsteps grabbed her attention.

Tristan's powerful form made its way across the flagstones of the pool area, his eyes unmoving from where she sat, like a laser focused upon its target. Nina sat up a little straighter in her seat, resisting the urge to run away and avoid him a little longer. He hadn't been able to hide his dissatisfaction last night, but she shouldn't be surprised. Would he be heartbreakingly kind and let her down easy? Would he pretend it never happened? She didn't know which was worse.

In the end he simply stood and glowered down at her once he reached the opposite end of the low table she sat at. His breath came heavily, as though perhaps he'd run some of the short distance from the villa.

'Good morning,' she said, her voice a slight croak when he continued to simply stare down at her without speaking. 'Did you…um…want some coffee?'

'What are you doing?' he said, his voice low and perilously near to a growl.

'I'm waiting for the photo shoot to begin. I like to be on time.'

His jaw worked for a second, his gaze moving to rove down over her bare legs and feet before he scrubbed a hand over his jaw. 'Have I woken up in some alternate dimension or did we not make love last night?'

'We did,' she said, steeling herself to simply lay it

all out there since he seemed hell-bent on doing so. 'If you're wondering why I left, I thought perhaps some space might be needed today, to avoid any uncomfortable conversations. As you can see, I'm completely fine and not going to spend the day crying or whatever you might think virgins do in the aftermath of being… deflowered, or whatever they call it now. I don't regret it and I don't want you to feel obligated to be kind to me.'

Tristan stared down at her, a muscle ticcing in his jaw. 'Nina, kindness is the bare minimum I should treat you with. *Dios*… I was simply taken off guard by your little…deception. But I see now that I wasn't careful enough with you. I didn't intend for you to feel you had to run away from me.'

She folded her arms across her chest. 'Deception? Is that how you view what happened last night?'

'You weren't completely honest with me. I could have hurt you, badly. I *did* hurt you.'

He had no idea how much he was still hurting her, she thought balefully as she felt a lump in her throat. Standing up suddenly, she resisted the urge to run and stood her ground, hands on hips. 'I may not have proclaimed my virginity from the rooftops, but I was not dishonest and I didn't deliberately deceive you. I expected someone of your vast experience to be able to read between the lines, that's all.'

'*Que?*' He paused, dark blond brows rising almost to his hairline. 'Are you saying that you blame *me* for what happened?'

Nina picked up her empty coffee cup and bowl, moving swiftly down the steps towards the castle, forcing him to keep pace with her. 'I don't see why blame has to be placed anywhere. We are two grown adults who had sex. It was all…perfectly fine and consensual.'

One moment she was racing ahead of him, the next he'd moved to block her way through the archway to the kitchen building with one muscled forearm. She looked up, finding his handsome face staring down at her with abject incredulity.

'Fine and consensual,' he echoed, eyes not leaving hers.

'Exactly.'

'So if I were to suggest we make it a regular thing, you'd slot me into your schedule?' He ran a hand along the side of her face, brushing aside an errant lock of hair. 'Tell me, Nina—which colour-coded category would sex with me fall into? Orange for social events? Or perhaps blue for personal well-being?'

'I'd probably say red for fitness regimen,' she snapped, praying he couldn't hear the rampant hammering of her heart as she tried desperately to appear as calm and controlled as possible.

He bared his teeth in a smile that still didn't quite meet his eyes. 'Ah, of course, we worked up quite a sweat, didn't we, *querida*? I'm glad I was of service to you, then.'

She blushed, turning her head away in an effort to escape this ridiculous game he was playing with her. He was angry about the whole virginity detail, that much was certain.

'It's irrelevant, because you made it perfectly clear from the start that we *won't* be making it a regular thing.

And for what it's worth I agree—it's best not to complicate our arrangement any further. Now, if you'll let me go, I need to go and have some cold pointy diamonds draped all over me.' She pushed at his chest to no avail, looking up to find him glaring at her, ice-blue eyes narrowed with tension. He licked his lips and for a moment she thought he might do something utterly ridiculous, like kiss her until she couldn't stand up. He could—they were still playing the part of blissful lovebirds, after all. But in the end, he simply gritted his jaw and moved aside.

He was being punished.

By whom, he wasn't quite sure. He had been the one to agree with Astrid that they use Nina for the jewellery campaign while they were here, after all. But as Nina walked back out onto set in the world's tiniest flesh-coloured two-piece swimming suit, draped in Falco diamonds, he rather felt as though he were being tortured.

Her tanned skin glowed under the late afternoon sun, with summer having finally decided to make an appearance. She didn't glance his way as she was shown around the set that took up most of the lavish stone courtyard, smiling and nodding as the team discussed the vintage car they'd be using for the day. A model that she was expected to pose upon while draped in Falco diamonds, the director had explained to him only moments before. His gut churned as he recalled the similar photo shoot she'd done in that magazine several years ago, but he forced himself to remain still, to not interfere.

She was not a damsel in need of rescuing, as she'd

told him. She had consented to act as a model, knowing full well what it might entail. But as she finally looked up and met his gaze, offering up a small polite wave before turning her back, he fought the urge to growl.

It wasn't that he'd expected clingy tears upon waking this morning, but when a man awoke after the most peaceful sleep of his life to find that his bed partner had already fled the scene after their interlude… It had got under his skin. He still felt completely on edge after last night, his ego and his control rubbed raw. For all of his grand ideas about maintaining their professionalism and distance in the wake of their lovemaking, he was the one having to refrain from jumping up, throwing her over his shoulder like a caveman and depositing her back into his bed for the rest of the afternoon.

As he watched, the director's assistant instructed her to move, draping the thin silk wrap she'd been provided with over her shoulders to cover her mostly naked flesh. She moved with ease, her athlete's muscles bunching up and flexing as she slid herself into place, perfectly following the direction. However, was he imagining the slight look of discomfort in her tightened features as she settled herself more fully upon the hard edge of the car's bonnet? When she moved again, the director's assistant sliding her a couple of inches to the right and removing her wrap again, she winced and readjusted herself.

Tristan's stomach tensed with awareness at the sudden possibility that she was uncomfortable with far more than just her body being on display. He'd been careless last night in bed with her; surely she would've told him if she was too sore to do the shoot today?

Even as the thought occurred to him he shrugged it off, knowing that was exactly what Nina would *not* do. She would insist upon working past her own limits, ignoring her own feelings, much too stubborn for her own good.

As the director called out for her to change position once again Nina's face tightened, and this time a low hiss escaped her lips before she straightened and posed once more.

He'd had enough.

'Cut!' he called out loudly. 'Stop everything. Stop.'

'What? We're in the middle of a take,' the director shouted, gesturing wildly with her hands.

'I need to speak with my fiancée,' he growled, striding across the set until he reached her side in a few short steps. Nina looked up at him, her arms crossed defensively over her chest. 'We haven't finished yet, Tristan. You can't just yell out cut because you wish to speak with me.'

'I can and I am,' he insisted. 'Be honest with me, please—are you in pain?'

Her mouth tightened, her gaze slipping to look away, past his shoulder. 'It's no more than I can handle. Go back to your chair.'

'Everyone, take an early lunch in town, my treat. My housekeeper will escort you.' He gripped her waist gently, lifting her slim weight up against his chest. 'You...come with me.'

Thankfully she didn't fight him when he insisted on draping her silk robe back around her shoulders and gathering her into his arms. The journey from the courtyard back to his villa was a blur as he fought the red haze of rage that had settled over him. Rage at his own PR team for suggesting that she model his diamonds when the focus should have been on her role as a woman in motorsport, rage at the magazine's decision to have her pose semi-nude, but most of all rage at himself for allowing it all to happen. Because he knew that he had put her in this situation, the same situation her parents had once put her in. He should know better.

When they finally entered his bedroom, she kicked her legs, fighting her way into a standing position before tightening the belt on the flimsy robe.

'I hope that you have a good explanation for why you just did that.' She stood, arms crossed, black eyes narrowed upon him like a furious queen.

The fact that she had been nicknamed with ice in mind was so utterly laughable, not only because he had experienced her fire first-hand, but because her passion and strength burned hotter than anything he had ever seen. His attraction to her was so much deeper than the quick sexual gratification she had accused him of pursuing.

'Tristan, you can't just shut down an expensive photo shoot with no explanation. People are going to talk and make assumptions.'

'Let them,' he said, scowling at her. 'I don't care about their opinions.'

'The whole point was to mingle our two families' brands and meet somewhere in the middle. Fashion and racing.' She shrugged one slim shoulder. 'I wouldn't have agreed to it if I didn't feel totally comfortable.'

'Did you?' He stepped closer. 'Because from where I was sitting you looked pretty damn uncomfortable.'

'Is that what this is about? Your conscience at hurting me last night? Because, honestly, I've heard that discomfort in those circumstances is pretty unavoidable. It really doesn't matter.'

'It matters to me,' he insisted, tightening his hold on her wrist and pulling her closer. 'You can act as unaffected as you like, but, from a purely physical point of view, I should've taken better care of you. I would have done it so much differently if I'd known.'

She paused, her gaze softening at his regret. 'You would have?'

'Oh, yes,' he said, inhaling a deep breath of her inimitable scent. 'I would have taken my time. I would have made it so much better for you. You have no idea how good it would have been.'

He ran his cheek against the soft skin of her neck, breathing her in and feeling her shiver in response. She was always so responsive, so honest. Perhaps that was why he'd flown into an immediate fury upon waking up alone in his bed this morning. Her scent had surrounded him, but her warmth had been long gone and the idea that she'd left him…that he might never get to touch her again… It had been unacceptable.

'Let me put this into terms you'll appreciate,' he murmured softly. 'You see, you expected the Falco experience, but I didn't have all the details. If I'd known exactly what I was going into, I would have changed my tactics and strategy in order to achieve the best result for you. Your pleasure is what's most important to me, and the sound of you in pain… I can't get it out of my mind. I need to replace it with the sound of your pretty moans as you come. With the sound of you calling out my name in ecstasy. I'm a perfectionist, *querida*, so please let me make this right.'

'You're not playing fair.' She gasped as his erection made contact with her hip.

He took her face into his hands, meeting her eyes. 'This isn't a game. Not here. There are no cameras, no audience to pretend to. Whatever this is from now on… It's just between me and you.'

CHAPTER TEN

IF THIS WAS a punishment of sorts, please sign her up. She wanted him never to stop.

He laid her back on the bed, kissing a path from her inner ankle up past her knee, slowing down all the more the closer he got to the apex of her thighs. Then, to her frustration, he moved to the top of the opposite thigh and began a slow path downwards again. At her whimper of discontent, he chuckled darkly.

He rose up onto his knees, gazing down at her with a look of what she hoped was deep admiration, but she couldn't quite tell. He got back into place between her thighs, sliding her underwear down slowly until she was fully bare to him. Smoothly, he sucked on his index finger, taking the glistening digit and sliding it down in a line between her intimate folds. Nina moaned as he began a slow silky torture between her thighs, until she practically begged him to insert that tricky finger. He refused of course, leaning down to blow cold air upon her tortured flesh.

'I told you, it's too soon for that. You need time to recover. This is just about making you feel good, Nina. I'm going to make you feel so good.'

Nina gasped as Tristan's lips pressed against her core, his fingers spreading her wide as he leaned in to kiss her silky hot skin. It felt absurdly intimate and intense and for a moment she wondered if she might push his head away, but as he licked and laved her just in the perfect spot she seemed to melt. Her body relaxed, mind emptying of all thoughts other than, *Yes!* and, *More!* and, *Please, Tristan, oh, please...*

After a time she realised that those words were actually escaping her own lips on small gasps and pleas for mercy as his gentle teasing kisses became more demanding. He worked her body as though he knew every inch of it. He was a master of pleasure, and she was fully at his mercy, coming apart at the seams.

The orgasm that built within her seemed to overtake her entire body, tuning her nerve endings to a fine point and then breaking her apart with an explosion of heat and wave after wave of delicious pleasure. After a few breathless moments of delirium, she regained an awareness of her surroundings and realised he hadn't made any move to continue as they had the night before.

'Still tender?' he murmured against her inner thigh, stroking a hand along her still sensitive skin and making her shiver.

She shook her head to signal no, because the ache in her core had shifted into something very different from the reminder of her first time. Her hips shifted against him, her throat working with the effort not to beg for the scorching stretch of relief that she craved.

Tristan's eyes darkened, seeing far too much as he rose to his knees above her on the bed. 'The crew will be returning from town soon…but I think we have time for a shower.'

'Together?' she asked, picturing the intimate slide of hands along wet flesh and feeling her cheeks heat.

His smile was devilish as he lifted his head, a man thoroughly satisfied with his work. 'This was a good start. But I'm going to need to gather more data if I'm expected to formulate an accurate strategy.'

'How much more?' she asked, trying not to show how ridiculously turned on his racing terminology made her when used in this context. It was perfect, he was perfect, and he wanted this just as much as she did. It was almost too perfect to believe, but she could worry over the potential risks and consequences later. Much later.

'As much as you can take, kitten. If you think you can handle me?'

A flush of arousal pooled low in her belly and she knew she was in trouble, but she'd always been powerless to resist a challenge. Tristan Falco was like the thrill of the track distilled into human form and if she wasn't careful, she'd lose herself in his wicked games.

She smiled back, her limbs heavy with pleasure as she accepted his hand and allowed him to lead her to the bathroom where he proceeded to show her exactly what kind of data he intended to gather from her until they were both weak limbed and thoroughly late to finish the rest of the photo shoot.

Over the course of the afternoon, Nina felt Tristan's eyes on her and her body seemed to be experiencing a constant low hum of awareness in his presence. If anything, it only enhanced her confidence for her poses. Usually she felt awkward and ridiculous during photo shoots like this, but with Tristan's gaze devouring her, she came alive.

The magazine photographer deferred often to Tristan's expertise and while he didn't actually take any photos of her himself, he did offer up some great ideas to change the direction from the earlier, more sexual poses to something edgier and infinitely more unique. He had an artist's eye, she realised as he instructed the crew to drive the car back into the long expanse of the garage for some of the shots and incorporate a stack of spare tyres and mechanical tools in the foreground to represent Nina's knowledge of the industry she loved.

As they gathered to see a preview of the photos, Nina felt surprisingly satisfied with looking at herself in the images. She looked powerful and sexy, as if the woman and the athlete had been given equal space to shine. The Falco Diamonds team also joined them for a few hours and were quick and efficient in completing their objectives for their campaign.

When Tristan announced that part of the Falco experience included being whisked away by him on a yacht for a couple of weeks, Nina found herself agreeing. She was technically still on bed rest, even if there might not be much resting being done while in bed with Tristan… But, for once, she allowed herself to play hooky from her strenuous schedule. After assuring Sophie that she would meet her in Argentina for the next race, she threw caution to the wind and accepted Tristan's invitation.

* * *

'I'm just saying—you definitely cheated,' Tristan growled, his breath still coming hard and fast in the wake of a late afternoon lovemaking session. Nina smiled, remembering how he'd reacted after she'd beaten him at chess for a fifth time and he'd responded by pinning her down and punishing her with kisses that had eventually devolved into them retreating to his master cabin for several hours.

'I never cheat,' she teased, rolling over to tuck herself into the side of his chest. 'You simply aren't up to my skill level yet. But don't worry, I'll be very gentle with you next time.'

'Little minx.' His laughter rumbled against her skin and she smiled at the easy intimacy they'd fallen into over the past few days spent alone. He'd taken a much smaller vessel out and insisted on only a skeleton crew to give them as much privacy as possible. It was as if they'd stepped into a dream.

Since they'd set sail on his yacht, the world's wildest playboy had thrown himself into showing her exactly how he had got his reputation. He made love to her in the morning as the dawn light crept into the opulent master cabin. He seduced her on the top deck in broad daylight after plying her with strawberries and champagne. The shameless man had even infiltrated her daily workout, in the gym filled with specialist equipment that he'd had inserted into the yacht specifically for her to use.

She couldn't complain though, because he was certainly keeping her in shape on her time off. With both their bedroom activities and the myriad excursions he arranged for them, like snorkelling off the coast of Corsica and a hiking trip along Sardinia's Montiferru mountain trail. For someone who'd travelled throughout much of Europe and beyond as a part of her job, she realised that she had been far too insular in how she spent her time away from the track. She ate at the same restaurants, walked the same paths and generally put all of her energy into driving all of the time. Even the few friendships she'd had had waned and dissipated since she'd removed herself from the public spectacle of being another Roux family scandal.

But spending time with Tristan felt like stepping into a dream, where none of that mattered. Sure, the sex was becoming addictive, but even more intoxicating were the moments where they simply spent time together, just existing. She'd told him more about her past, her relationship with her parents and how they'd barely spoken to one another—or to her and Alain—since her mother had remarried. In turn, Tristan had shared his experiences of growing up with a single mother and his regret at never having the opportunity to know his father, who had died shortly after Dulce had discovered she was expecting him.

As well as personal conversations, they didn't shy away from talking about work, with Tristan surprisingly eager to discuss his ideas for the future of Falco Roux and her usually countering with how he was entirely wrong. He respected her expert opinion, she'd quickly realised, and so she eventually felt safe to share with him her belief that their management team was riddled with misogyny and inequality. He'd been furious that night, their peaceful meal at an Italian marina derailed while he'd asked for more details and had taken notes of names.

The whole thing had made her feel strange but relieved that she'd spoken up and that she hadn't been immediately shot down. Tristan was aware of his privilege as team owner and as a man among men and, even long after she'd settled him down with kisses and caresses back in the comfort of their quiet cabin on the yacht, she'd caught moments of unrest in him as he'd stared broodily out at the ocean.

After that day, she'd steered clear of any more talk of Falco Roux, trying to redirect him towards more playful avenues of entertainment. Hence why, today, she'd suggested they play chess. He knew only how to play at a basic level, so naturally she had beaten him time after time. But he was an entertaining opposition. He was not a sore loser; he threw himself into the game and into the mental back-and-forth that he seemed to intuitively know she enjoyed most.

But even as she lay in the wake of their lovemaking and tried to tell herself to relax and enjoy this temporary break for what it was, the reality of their situation was always looming on the horizon like an elephant in the room that neither of them wished to address first. Lying in bed with him like this, she felt as if she were just waiting for the other shoe to drop. For something to ruin this interlude and remind her of all the reasons why it would only end in heartbreak.

But no, that wasn't possible because her heart most definitely was not involved. She tended to get overly attached to people sometimes when she really liked them, that was all. It was just infatuation and endorphins from amazing sex. Maybe that was why she had begun to day-dream about floating down the aisle in a flowing white gown. No amount of chemistry and infatuation would change the fact that this wasn't a real engagement and there would be no real wedding bells chiming in their future. She was too young and too busy with her ca-reer dreams to be having such absurd thoughts. Right?

'You seem preoccupied,' he murmured, pulling her closer against him. 'I thought I'd worked hard enough there to calm your mind for a bit.'

'Nothing calms my mind,' she said honestly. 'I only ever get a brief respite before it's right back to full speed again.'

'Sounds exhausting.' He chuckled. 'But it makes sense.'

'How so?' She turned to look up at him.

'You couldn't do the job you do without an enormous amount of focus and knowledge. You're talented and you work hard, of course, but you're also gifted, from what I can tell. You don't just know the sport, you live and breathe it.'

She hesitated for a moment, then decided to tell him what she'd begun to suspect about herself. She told him about what she'd learned of autism and neurodivergence and how it often ran in families for generations unde-tected for a variety of reasons. By the time she realised she'd been talking uninterrupted for far too long, she felt a little ridiculous and poised to apologise and change the subject, only for Tristan to surprise her once again.

'I can see it.' He smiled, one hand smoothing down

over her hair. 'The way your mind works has fascinated me from the moment we met. Like you see the world in high definition, no detail missed. But I can see how that would be an intense way to live.'

Nina sat with the strange feeling of being finally *seen* and tried to repress the emotion that had filled her chest. There was no way he could know what just listening and validating her wild new feelings and thoughts would mean to her, but even if he was just being kind…it was more than she'd ever experienced before.

'I think I've always been different in a way no one around me could understand,' she said quietly. 'Except maybe my brother. He's different too, in his own way. He knows just as much as me about racing, and he even got a seat after the academy at eighteen. But where I thrived with the consistency and the heavy workload, he struggled and turned to partying to cope. He couldn't keep up with the pressure to perform in Elite One, so they let him go.'

Tristan seemed to stiffen at the mention of her brother, his gaze slipping away from her as they listened to the peaceful lapping of waves on the outside of the yacht.

'Alain is a troubled soul,' he offered vaguely.

'He is. I think that's when he started to lose control. He wanted to join the R&D team, maybe be team principal someday. But he felt ashamed of not living up to the family name or something. And then I started doing so well in my racing…' She frowned, thinking of her own single-minded nature and how obsessed she'd been with graduating top of the academy. Had she ever asked her brother how he was? 'I don't think I was a very good sister to him.'

'You can't blame yourself for the actions and struggles of the people you love. Trust me, that way lies only suffering.' Tristan sighed, seemingly agitated by her admission. 'Your brother is a grown man. He will either figure it out, or he won't. Either way, none of that is on you.'

'Spoken like someone with a similar experience?' she asked, curious.

For a moment she saw a strange emotion cross his features, and his throat worked as though he was about to speak before he stopped himself. 'I won't pretend to know why your brother did the things he's done. Just as I had to admit the same about my uncle. He became severely depressed after his wife, my aunt, died of cancer; he became disassociated from the estate and impossible to reach emotionally by those closest to him, and, with his refusal to help himself, he left a lot of people hurt and angry in the process. In the end, his total immersion in his grief to the exclusion of all else killed him, and nearly took me with him. I couldn't save him, nor could my mother or Victor. I don't think anyone could.'

'You're very wise, Tristan Falco,' she mused, running a hand along his chest.

'Is that your way of calling me old?' He growled, pulling her on top of him. And just like that, they both made a silent agreement to avoid the darker turn that their conversation had taken and throw themselves back into the fantasy of it just being the two of them alone in their bubble. And while Nina was grateful, she still couldn't shake the feeling that something had shifted between them, that the path ahead had become infinitely more perilous.

CHAPTER ELEVEN

BY THE TIME the day came for them to travel with the team to Buenos Aires, Nina found herself wishing for more time off for the first time ever. Usually, she hated the three-week vacation that took place in the middle of each Elite One season, but this one, now more than halfway through, was possibly the most enjoyable holiday she'd ever had. Tristan was fun and charming and educated, and while having sex with him was rather amazing, even by her very inexperienced standards, conversation with him was just as stimulating. It was a pity reality ever had to intrude.

The commercial jet that Tristan had chartered for their entire team to travel upon together was top of the range and included a handful of private cabins for the owner and the management of the team, along with the three drivers travelling together. From the moment they'd boarded the jet, Apollo and Daniele Roberts had disappeared into their cabins. As had the team principal and the other members of the board who were travelling with them. Nina had brought her things into her own cabin area and then immediately gone in search of Tristan, who had gone to speak with the pilot. When he re-entered his cabin to find her sitting upon his make-shift bed, he did not look as seductive and relaxed as he had when they'd awoken upon the yacht earlier this morning. Instead, he had a tightness about him.

'Is everything okay?'

He nodded, putting his hands into the pockets of his trousers, then taking them back out again to place them upon his hips and stare around the small cabin walls. He looked rather like a lion in captivity, she thought, as if he were pacing behind the bars of his cage and wishing to be anywhere but here.

She had never considered the fact that flying might be difficult for him, considering his accident. It was hard to see past the calm, confident mask that he portrayed to the world. Surely he would have told her...but as she thought back, there was no denying he avoided flying. In all their time together, he had opted for private train cars, yacht travel, he had even driven for hours on end in lieu of the much faster option of helicopters or jets.

'Do you struggle with air travel?' she asked gently, standing up to place one hand on his chest.

'I manage okay.'

'Tristan.'

'Nina, I don't need your pity right now.' The words came out of his mouth harshly, and she tried not to take offence. He was feeling whatever he was feeling and she wouldn't judge.

'Let me help.'

A small laugh escaped his lips, and he scrubbed his hand over the stubble upon his jaw before finally meeting her eyes. 'Nothing helps. The terror is the same every time. The memories, the intrusive thoughts... It feels just like it did... That day.'

'The day of your accident,' she finished for him.

'Yes, the day of the...crash.' He inhaled, releasing his breath slowly before lowering himself down into the seat opposite hers.

Nina leaned forward, placing both of her hands upon his knees and squeezing gently. 'That must be an incredibly difficult thing to manage, all by yourself.'

He nodded once as he stared determinedly at the window. 'I didn't remember much of the accident itself for weeks afterwards, a temporary blackout of sorts. It's quite common, apparently. But I had dreams, and in the dreams... I heard the noise of the engines getting louder, the sounds of screaming, the rushing of wind. Everything after that... I lost. I woke up in a hospital bed with my mother sobbing by my side telling me that my uncle was gone. For a long time what I felt was anger. And a lot of confusion as to why I'd survived when he hadn't. I was young, selfish and more expendable than he was in the grand scheme of things.'

'You survived something truly terrible. That's not something anyone could predict or control.'

'Therapy helped me to see that eventually. I've worked through every stage of grief in the past decade but eventually I decided to help myself and step up within the Falco company and take the reins. But the flying... Still brings me to my knees every time.'

Her heart ached for the brave man in front of her and the senseless pain that he'd been put through. Life could be so unimaginably cruel sometimes, but she felt such relief that he had survived that accident. She would guess his mother felt the same relief too. As the pilot came online to say they were about to take off, Tristan closed his eyes.

'Let me stay with you?' she asked gently. Knowing that if he asked her to leave, she would.

'Please,' he said simply.

That one word lit up something in her chest, warming her through as she took the seat alongside him and they both did up their belts. As the plane ascended, Tristan's breathing became laboured but his hand didn't drop hers. She remained silent by his side as he worked through it at his own pace, not rushing him or trying to guide his panic. Just letting him be.

When a flight attendant came to interrupt them, Nina politely shooed them away, placing the 'do not disturb' sign upon the outside of the cabin door, and waited.

Tristan became aware of his surroundings in flashes of colour. The white of the closed cabin door. The blue of his jeans. The dark curtain of Nina's soft hair as she leaned over him and wrapped him in her embrace. He pulled her onto his lap, tightening his grip on her as he inhaled and exhaled deeply.

As the panic faded, there was only her. Only Nina. She peppered his face with kisses, gentle at first, but quickly he felt her breath hitch and her hips jerk.

'Is this still a part of your plan to distract me?' he asked.

She laughed against his cheek as he trailed his own

kisses down the side of her neck, but he felt the speed of her arousal in her heartbeat against his lips.

'I've clearly unleashed a sex-mad woman, *mi amor.*'

The endearment slipped from his lips as smoothly as air and he felt her stiffen momentarily, her eyes gliding to his in a question he answered quickly with a deeper, much more demanding kiss. His heart hammered in his chest, not with anxiety but with the utter unpractised uncertainty that came with every interaction with this maddening woman. She made him feel godlike and uncertain all at once.

'You just *love* to flatter yourself,' she breathed, fighting to hide a groan as his hands cupped her breasts through the stretch material of her T-shirt.

'Tut-tut. Always fighting me.' He smacked one palm lightly upon her behind in faux punishment. 'Why do you have to wear such sensible clothing?'

'You'd prefer if I walked onto the plane in a diamond-encrusted thong?'

'If I had it my way, you'd never be clothed. Ever.'

'That might get in the way of safety regulations when I drive.'

The reminder of her safety, of her career, made him want to hold onto her even tighter. It made him feel as if he was losing control all over again, only this time it had nothing to do with his traumatic past and everything to do with the very perfect, very alive woman straddling him. He leaned his head between her breasts, fighting off the urge to make demands he knew he had no right to make.

'What are you thinking?' she whispered, her soft, perfect lips tracing a path along the side of his neck.

'I'm just thinking, these tight-fitting yoga pants pose a challenge to the very despicable things I want to do to you. A challenge...but not an impossible one.'

He showed her just how very possible it could be, while the hum of the jets coupled with the closed cabin door provided just enough privacy to conceal her loud groan as she sank down onto his length. Her eyes met his in innocent question as she tested her movements and he was reminded once again how new she was to this. How he was the only person who ever had seen her this way, so wild and hungry for release. How it made him feel possessive, as though he'd stumbled upon a rare gem in the rubble and he needed to keep it all for himself.

Dios, she was...unmatched. And he was becoming completely undone just by looking at her as she braced her hands on his chest and began to grind her perfect body over him. The pressure of keeping quiet made everything more intense and he lost control at the exact moment she came apart.

Afterwards, he kept her on his lap, his hands stroking through her hair as she asked questions about his home city of Buenos Aires, about his family and his childhood. He knew she was still distracting him, but he was grateful for it as he described his father's close-knit family and how they compared with the much more crusty, upper-class Falco clan. How the world had reacted when Dulce Falco had recently announced her engagement and upcoming wedding after decades of being a content widow. How, in the wake of his public cuckolding by Victor and Gabriela, Dulce had decided that match-making was all the support he needed. His mother had always been a big character in his life and something warmed within him when Nina openly chuckled at his description of the recent bizarre and hilarious match-making attempts he'd endured at his mother's behest.

'It makes sense now, why you needed a fake fiancée so quickly,' she mused, the aftermath of her mirth still spilling from the corner of her smiling eyes.

'Yes, but she will demand the real thing soon enough. She's found love again and has settled into retirement so naturally she's now decided I have to give her the big society wedding and the grandchildren she craves. Getting married herself clearly isn't enough.'

Nina stilled in his arms, her lips curving down. 'What about what you want?'

'I made my mother a promise that I would settle down this year, mostly just to stop her worrying about me.' He shrugged. 'But the more I think of it, the more I realise my playboy days had become less and less fun even before the drama with my cousin. Maybe…the reason why I've not fought back on this is because, deep down, I think I want it too.'

His own words hit him with the weight of truth he couldn't bear to look at too closely, not when he had just come down from the adrenaline of the past hour of anxiety and connection and openness. It was all suddenly too much and yet not nearly enough as he gathered Nina closer into his embrace and urged her to sleep. His exhausted mind drifted off quickly, where he was joined in his dreams by a bride that bore a striking resemblance to a certain raven-haired racing driver.

CHAPTER TWELVE

As a town car drove them through the heart of Buenos Aires, Nina fought off the waves of anxiety that made her chest feel tight and her skin prickle. Preparing to attend Dulce Falco's wedding and be introduced to Tristan's entire extended family as his fiancée was quite a jolt back to the reality of their ruse after the past two weeks spent in a bubble of their sensual explorations. Tristan had reassured her more than once that his family would be too thrilled to meet her to suspect the truth, but she was less certain.

On the yacht, it had been only them and the insatiable attraction between them. But from the moment they landed and the Falco family's small army of assistants appeared with a change of formal clothing for them both, she was reminded that she was very much expected to play a role here in front of people who knew Tristan the best—and she was no actress.

He'd told her they had the wedding's formal rehearsal dinner to attend the moment they landed, but still she hadn't been quite prepared for the level of pomp and circumstance surrounding his arrival back into the city. It had been a number of years since he'd visited Argentina, he'd explained quietly as they'd landed, and she'd looked out of the jet window to spy a small crowd of people had lined up around the fence of the runway of the private airfield. If she'd thought Tristan Falco was famous in Europe, it appeared he had an even more god-like status in his home country.

She'd taken her time donning the stretch satin golden sheath gown she'd been given along with matching gold diamond earrings and necklace. The material was a perfect fit, soft and seamless, and she'd smiled, knowing Tristan must have passed along her specifications. When she'd emerged back out onto the main area of the jet, Tristan had been fully dressed in a sleek black tuxedo and talking through their event schedule with his family's event co-ordinator. He'd seemed distracted as they'd been brought out to the limousine, even as he'd taken a moment to compliment her ensemble before being interrupted once again with some details about the wedding ceremony they would attend the following afternoon.

They hadn't actually discussed the parameters of their deal, now that they'd ventured into spending each night in one another's arms. Once the season ended and their three months were up, would she leave the team and become a stranger to him once more? The realisation that he still intended to fulfil his mother's wish of finding a bride and having a grand wedding had been a stark one on their flight over and she'd spent hours trying not to think of it after Tristan had fallen asleep.

He would find someone easily once she was gone, that much was for certain. But as for her…she couldn't quite imagine herself ever falling into another man's arms without comparing them to him. To her first lover. Over the past two weeks, something within her had begun to change and unravel. She'd begun skipping workouts and training exercises in favour of spending as much time as she could in Tristan's arms. Instead of mulling over circuit layouts and strategies when her mind was idle, she thought about midnight-blue eyes and how his smile lines transformed his entire face when he laughed.

Armed with a wardrobe of gowns for the handful of events over the coming days, Nina reminded herself to be on her guard. The Falco family were the highest of Buenos Aires society, and not only were they old money but they were also fiercely traditional people, which she found out quickly upon being introduced to his grand-mother, Valentina, his mother, Dulce, and his soon-to-be stepfather, Agustin, at the extravagant rehearsal dinner being held at an opulent hotel in the heart of the city.

'You are a racing driver?' Valentina asked her shrewdly, holding her hand and looking at her face as though trying to peer into her very soul. 'That little hobby will have to stop after the wedding.'

Nina stiffened, looking up at Tristan beside her as he coughed and immediately intervened.

'Abuela, Nina is very prominent in the motorsport world. It's not a hobby. It's her career,' he explained gently.

The older woman tutted. 'That's too dangerous a ca-reer for the mother of your children, my love.' And with that, the elderly woman walked away.

Tristan looked down at her with a wince. 'I love my

family, but you see now why I don't come home very often?' He laughed.

She attempted a laugh of her own, but the interaction shook her. And she felt even more on guard as she was introduced to the rest of the family one by one. His mother was a face she had seen countless times while growing up; Dulce Falco was a worldwide fashion icon. But here in her home city, surrounded by her loved ones, she wore very little make-up and a simple flowing gown of white linen embroidered with traditional Argentinian artwork. She looked rested and peaceful, the antithesis of the sleek, professional fashion mogul that had dominated fashion magazines and social pages for the previous four decades.

'So, this is the woman who has finally stolen my son's heart,' Dulce pronounced as she pulled Nina into a full hug. 'You are just as beautiful in person as you look whizzing around that racetrack. I've watched your last couple of raccs out of interest, and I've got to say—you are ferocious.'

Nina blushed. 'Coming from you, that's a huge compliment.'

Dulce waved a hand at the flattery, raising a brow in her son's direction. 'So ferocious, in fact, that I wonder why a certain team owner hasn't ensured that you are the one to lead Falco Roux to victory in this Argentinian Premio race.'

'Mama, we just landed. At least let a man eat before you begin taking him apart piece by piece.' Tristan sighed dramatically, then smirked and grabbed his mother in a deep hug.

Nina watched the open affection between mother and son and felt a twinge of jealousy. Any hugs or praise she'd ever received as a child had been veiled in expectation or judgment or had been a simple show for the press. Her parents had been selfish people, driven by their own individual agendas, and watching Tristan interacting with his own family now she could see the difference in how she had been treated. She had always just assumed that every family had their issues, but perhaps her own had been a little more problematic than she'd realised. Perhaps she was a little more affected than she'd realised too.

Much to Tristan's grandmother's horror, his mother insisted that Nina and Tristan sleep together in his childhood room once they all returned to the Falco family's grand town house after the evening of spectacular food and schmoozing was done.

Well, they described it as a *room* but, in fact, it was more of a penthouse apartment with a master bedroom and a study and a living room that overlooked the entire city of Buenos Aires. With jet lag weighing heavy upon her, she welcomed Tristan's suggestion that they go straight to bed. But as she followed him slowly into the master bedroom, she found herself pausing in the doorway.

'What's wrong?' he asked, frowning in the middle of removing his bow tie.

There was nothing wrong, of course. This entire day, the entire past two weeks, had been perfect, but with every moment she spent in his life and in his bed as his fake fiancée the lines of protection she'd drawn around her own heart grew thinner and thinner.

'I just wonder…if perhaps we should sleep separately.'

'And why would we do that?' He took a step towards her, his handsome features tightening with concern. 'Do you *want* to sleep separately?'

'No, of course not.' She shook her head.

He reached her side in a few easy strides, his hands sliding up her bare arms and coming to rest upon her cheeks. 'Then let's not,' he murmured against her lips. 'I feel like I've barely touched you since we landed, and we've barely had a moment alone. I've been counting down the moments till I had you all to myself again. Sleep here, where you belong. With me.'

She ignored how his words made something deep within her chest sing with joy, telling herself that he simply meant he didn't wish to sleep alone. Truthfully, neither did she. She'd thought about it over and over and if she had to choose between ending this now for the sake of self-preservation or risking her heart for a few more weeks of pleasure, she'd choose the latter. Even if it hurt, at least she'd know she had him, even just for a little while.

'There won't be much sleeping if I'm in bed with you.' She laughed, then gasped as his lips slid down to the most sensitive part of her neck.

'Get into bed, let me debauch you a little. Then you can sleep.'

And so she did, ignoring the alarm bells going off in her mind as she imagined this was a real love affair and her real fiancé was making love to her in his childhood bedroom while they tried to keep quiet. She let Tristan's touch still her overactive mind as his attempt at letting her sleep turned into slow, languorous lovemaking that carried on well into the night.

Tristan walked his mother down the aisle to marry the man she loved so dearly, who had made her so happy, and was proud to say that only the smallest tear slid down his cheek as he placed his mother's hands into the shaking one of his stepfather. Agustin leaned across and placed a kiss upon his stepson's cheek, whispering words of thanks into his ear. As Tristan sat down beside Nina, she quickly gripped his hand in hers and he realised that she too was feeling the emotion as his mother gave an impassioned speech about the longevity of love and how short people's time together in this world was.

The celebration that followed was one of the grandest that their home had ever seen and Tristan revelled in having all of his relations together under one roof. They feasted like kings, with a famous local chef having been hired to create a unique twist on the traditional wedding buffet of *carne asada*, roasted pigs and freshly prepared fish. *Empanadas*, *provoleta* and *chimichurri* were also in abundance, along with copious bottles of the famous Falco reserve Malbec, some of which Nina sampled with gusto despite technically still being deep in her training regime as a reserve for the race the following weekend.

After Dulce and Agustin completed a beautiful first dance, they urged Tristan and Nina to join them and what followed was possibly the most hilarious attempt at instructing his fiancée in the Argentine tango. She begged him to stop, but eventually devolved into laughter as he careened her around the dance floor to the tune of the band's dramatic music. Their guests laughed heartily at the display, and as he looked down into Nina's sparkling eyes, he was helpless to do anything except capture her lips in a deep kiss. She kissed him back, despite the loud tutting from his grandmother, and his mother whooped loudly with delight.

When his stepfather asked to take Nina for a dance, Tristan took his mother to sit down and rest her weary feet. He guided her to the side of the open-air dance floor, where they sat together and Tristan watched as Nina bravely attempted a simple waltz.

'Good thing her driving isn't impeded by her two left feet.' His mother laughed good-naturedly.

Tristan smiled. 'She's making a great attempt though, to her credit. She's a perfectionist, so admitting her faults is hard for her. I'm not sure she knows she doesn't have many of them, though.'

He turned to find his mother looking at him with a strange smile on her face.

'I was going to wait until my wedding festivities were over to have this conversation with you, but I see now that I should probably just get it out of the way.'

'What's wrong?' Tristan asked.

'Nothing, at least I hope not. When you told me you were engaged to a woman I'd never heard you mention to me, or even seen you photographed with, naturally I was a little suspicious. So I did some digging... And

I discovered your little PR dilemma and realised what you'd done in coming up with this little deception.'

Tristan frowned. 'You did, did you?'

'I know you better than anyone. I know when something is off…so, you see, I was preparing myself for your acting skills—and hers too. I'd already written my speech, about why lying to your mother in her old age is a despicable act, even if I knew you'd have some kind of ridiculously guilt-ridden good intentions at heart.'

'Mama.' Tristan turned in his seat, wanting to explain himself.

She raised her hand to stop him, then placed it firmly upon his knee, meeting his eyes. 'My son, I was waiting to see how far you would go with this ruse just to please me. But now that I've seen you together, I can see that you've dug yourself into a much deeper hole than you had intended.'

'I don't know what you mean.'

She smiled knowingly, looking up as her new husband twirled Nina in a circle and her laugh rang out across the dance floor. 'I think you know exactly what I mean, darling. She's perfect for you. You are both so madly in love with each other. I think perhaps we should have saved today's wedding for you.'

Tristan thought about the idea of walking Nina down the aisle today, while his entire family looked on. The sensation in his chest was one of absolute primal possession and the need to see that happen. Was it true? Had he fallen in love with his fake fiancée? He, the wildest playboy, a man utterly allergic to commitment… But then again that wasn't *quite* true, was it? He had never openly courted the idea of settling down, but he hadn't been averse to it, once upon a time.

It was only since watching his beloved uncle deteriorate into a man he didn't recognise, and seeing the utter devastation that came with losing the one you loved, that Tristan had made some kind of subconscious decision not to forge any more connections of his own in case he got just as badly hurt. Not even Gabriela had touched his heart that deeply. He realised now that it had been only his pride that was stung by her and Victor's betrayal.

'Tristan... I want you to be happy. You deserve a great love just like the one that I once had with your father. And like the one I have now, since I finally let myself be loved again. I've watched you hide yourself away over the past decade since your uncle's death, blaming yourself for not being able to reach him through his depression, and trying to put yourself in a glass cage of sorts, where your heart could be seen but not touched by anyone.'

'Mama, please let's not talk about this today.'

'If not today, then when?' she asked firmly. 'I lost my brother that day, just as you lost your father figure, but ever since then I've felt like I've only had half of you too. Then Gabriela and Victor dented your smile even more, and I could have killed them. I didn't invite them here today because I thought it would be painful for you. I want you to know that you matter most to me and even though you keep telling me you're fine, I know you. But now, this beautiful girl...she's reawakened something within you that's been lost for a long time, my love. She's brought you back to life.'

His mother's words rang in his ears long after the dancing had come to an end and their guests had begun to filter out. Soon, the only ones left were him and Nina, all alone in the dim lighting as the servers moved to clear away the chairs and tables.

'We should go up too,' Nina said, her cheeks still pink from the exertion of her night's dancing attempts. She wore a spectacular gown in deep red, a gown made for tango, and so when the low strains of music filtered up from a speaker in the main house, he pulled her close for one last dance of his own.

'You look beautiful,' he whispered against her cheek, sliding them into an easy movement.

'You're not so bad yourself.' She laughed, sighing when he dipped her back in the lamplight in a classic tango pose. 'I wish I were better at this. I wish I could do it for real.'

She was talking about the dance, of course, but something in Tristan's chest tightened at her words and what they evoked within him. 'You can…if you take a chance.'

'I think it has more to do with practice and skill.' She raised a brow.

He rolled her over his arm, stepping around her and pulling her back up against his chest. 'This is a dance about trust, about passion.'

'And speed and precision too, surely,' she argued, her foot stepping squarely upon his and making him wince.

'That too.' He chuckled, lowering her slowly over his arm so that her back arched and her breath caught. 'But mostly…it's about giving in to your deepest desires…letting go of all restraint and trusting your partner enough to catch you when you do.'

They stood for a long moment in the pose, with Nina's eyes not leaving his as he slowly pulled her back up to standing.

'I want to let go,' she whispered softly. 'I want to believe that I can…that it won't just lead me to a path of regrets. But I've never been a good partner…in the dance, I mean.'

He looked into her eyes, knowing that she hadn't just been talking about the dance, just as he hadn't either. But he couldn't think of the right words to say without sounding entirely mad. Trust me, Nina. Stay with me. Marry me.

He closed his eyes, remembering how important her racing career was to her, how she'd said she never wanted to be seen as a society princess, like her mother. She was still young, quite a bit younger than him. He had been her first lover, for goodness' sake. Marriage and motherhood were likely long-term goals for her, if they were even on her radar at all. Surely he was being selfish by wanting to keep her?

Not to mention he had yet to reveal the truth behind his deal with her brother. Non-disclosure agreement or not, he had to be fully honest with her if he had any chance of proposing they keep their arrangement going past the end of the season. Would she ever be able to forgive him for keeping secrets from her? Would she understand why he'd done it and that it had been the only way to save the Roux company from bankruptcy and complete collapse? He'd stayed silent, according to the conditions of the NDA, but it had become increasingly difficult as the guilt had started eating him up inside. And now he'd run out of time.

But he had to try. He had to hope that once Nina understood the full implications of his actions, she'd forgive him. Because he knew now with full certainty that, despite everything standing against them, it was the only thing he wanted.

He wanted Nina Roux in his life for real.

The Falco Aerodrome was an impressive new circuit that had been purpose-built for this year's Elite One Premio race by Tristan himself, which he proudly talked her through as they took a tour of the paddock. Nina had noticed that Tristan had seemed extra attentive in the two days since the wedding, but she'd put it down to the abundance of amazing sex they'd been having. But with the race now only a few days away, she knew she had to get back to her routine as soon as possible and try to regain her focus.

When Tristan was called into a meeting up in the executive boardrooms, she took the chance to take a tour of the Falco Roux garages where their team had already begun to set up in preparation for the upcoming race weekend. She was in the middle of inspecting an upgrade she'd overseen on their engine injection system when footsteps pounded down the tarmac outside and a man appeared in her peripheral vision. She stood up, expecting to see one of their mechanics, but instead froze with recognition.

Her brother stood in the entryway of the garage, his

dark hair and eyes so like her own as he looked awkwardly around before stepping inside.

'Alain.' She gasped in shock. 'What…what are you doing here?'

'Falco stopped answering my calls, and I needed to speak to you about this in person.'

Her stomach tightened at the look on her brother's face, all elation at seeing him melting away. He wasn't here to apologise to her for what he'd done or even to cheer their team on. He was here with the exact same look on his face as he'd had on the day when he'd told her about the sale of the Roux company.

'What would you need to speak to Tristan about?' she said coldly. 'You already walked away from all of this, Alain. You abandoned ship.'

Alain sighed heavily, running a hand through his hair in a gesture that reminded her so much of their father. He was like him in many ways.

'He hasn't told you anything about the deal we made yet, has he?'

'I know how easily you sold our family company to him for a tidy sum, practically bankrupting me in the process. I trusted you. I thought you were trying to save the company, not ruin it.'

Alain shook his head, a hollow laugh escaping his lips. 'I never went to him with the intention of selling. We were going to go bankrupt whether I sold or not. You have to believe that I wanted to save our family's legacy, Nina. Your legacy. I know I've made so many mistakes.'

'Understatement of the year,' Nina muttered.

'You're angry at me, and that's fair. But I'm not the

man you knew any more—the party boy, the wastrel. My recovery has taught me to accept the consequences of my actions and I guess now is the time I start doing that.'

Recovery? The consequences of his actions? Who on earth was this man and where was her brother? 'What are you not telling me?'

'The company was in bad shape when I took over from dad, but I made it all worse. I got into serious debt, Nina. Gambling debt. I refused to admit that I had a problem, until I got into a very high-stakes poker game with Tristan Falco.' Alain shook his head, walking as if to go towards the small bar at the wall before turning away with a hiss of breath. 'Old habits…'

Nina looked at her brother then, really looked at him and saw how much weight he'd lost since she'd last seen him. He looked…healthy. Not like a man who'd been partying on a yacht in the Mediterranean for the entire summer. His eyes were clear, he was clean-shaven and well dressed and, above all, he appeared sober.

Much like with their mother and father, the tradition of excessive partying, including drinking and gambling, among other vices, was not generally spoken of in their family. Nothing was mentioned other than clothing styles and newspaper articles and how they appeared to the outside world. They were a rotten apple with the prettiest, shiniest skin.

'That was my rock-bottom, Nina. I bet our family company in a poker game.'

'How could that be true? How would no one know?'

'Because Tristan took pity on me. He agreed to stage

it as a takeover, and we signed a non-disclosure agreement to keep it all under wraps. He gave me a year to sort myself out. He cut a deal, to freeze our shares while he took control of the majority and worked on bringing the company back to solvency. He always intended to give it back.'

She reared back, totally shocked. 'Why would he do that?'

'I still don't know. He said he had a sentimental attachment to the brand.'

Instantly she recalled the garage full of Roux motorcars his uncle had collected, and she ran an agitated hand through her hair.

Alain was still talking. 'I think the guy just has a hero complex, to be quite honest. Who was I to argue? Don't look a gift horse in the mouth and all that. He got me into a discreet programme. There is an island off Greece that's notorious for helping wealthy addicts get clean while also forcing us back to our humble roots. I've cleaned beaches, I've power-washed streets, I've helped the homeless… At some point I finally accepted that I am an addict and that I always will be, but that doesn't make me a lost cause.'

She felt a painful tweak at what he'd been struggling with. 'Alain, I never thought you were a lost cause. I know we fought but that doesn't mean I don't still love you.'

'Nina, please, this isn't even the beginning of me making amends with you. I was so selfish. I don't know how our parents didn't ruin you too, but you are such a good person. You didn't deserve any of that.'

'Neither did you.'

That simple, brief acknowledgement of their shared childhood pain felt like a knife sliding out from her ribs a few inches. She knew that there was more to be said between them, much more, but perhaps here and now was not the time. She still had to wrap her head around what Tristan had done...and what he'd been keeping from her.

'Why tell me now?'

'I saw the rumours of your engagement to Falco on social media and I just saw red. I don't understand what kind of game he's playing with you, but as soon as I could leave Greece, I had to come. To protect you.'

She looked over Alain's shoulder to see Tristan striding towards them, a stunned look on his face. Tristan, the man who had been lying to her all along... Or perhaps she'd simply been lying to herself about the kind of man she'd thought he was? She felt like such a fool. Excusing herself to Alain, she took the coward's way out and fled.

CHAPTER THIRTEEN

NINA WALKED QUICKLY away from the garage until she found herself wandering along the path that lined the empty racing track. She didn't even know where she was going, she just needed her body to move so that her mind could work through her own confusion. A hand landed upon her shoulder and she spun around with a squeak. Tristan stood before her, his face a mask of pain.

'You're running away without even allowing me a chance to explain?'

She could have said yes, because she needed time to think, to try to understand why he would have lied to her about her own brother's actions and how he'd come to be their team owner. But instead she felt the embarrassing build-up of tears in her eyes. 'You lied to me.'

'I was waiting to tell you myself,' he began, then stopped. 'I'm sorry. I wanted to tell you so many times, believe me. But apart from the legal agreements we signed, I also wanted to give your brother time and privacy to recover, as he'd asked.'

'I just don't understand any of it.' She shook her head. 'You knew you were lying to me about my brother. And yet you still kept it from me. You knew that he planned to come back once he'd recovered and take back the helm of the company himself, and yet you were about to let me accept a deal from Accardi and leave Falco Roux!'

'I would have told you before you took any deal from that licentious old man. Even despite the non-disclosure agreement I made with your brother, I intended to find a way to tell you the truth before you actually left Falco Roux. I only signed Apollo for the rest of this season, thinking it was the right thing to do for the team. I assumed your brother would want to make the decisions about his own drivers when he took over again.'

'You can see why I find that hard to believe, right?'

'That's fair.'

'None of this is fair. I'm so sick of this. I'm so unbelievably sick of having my future decided upon by men who have assumed all the power behind my back. I'm so sick of working so hard *all the time* and ending up right back where I started. I trusted you.'

He took a step towards her, closing the space between them. 'You can still trust me. I made a mistake. Regardless of the NDA, I should have told you sooner, I see that now. But your brother insisted that you not know. Don't let this ruin what we've started between us, Nina. I meant it for the best, to try and help save your family company. I want to make this work. Us. I want to earn your trust back and show you just how serious I am about never breaking it again.'

She bowed her head, wanting that explanation to be enough. But deep inside her, something had split apart at his deception. He'd known far more about Alain than he'd admitted. He'd known he was only caretaking the

Roux company until Alain was better. He'd seen how upset she'd been about being forced out of a main driver's seat, and, despite him erroneously thinking that signing a more experienced driver for the rest of this season was the right thing to do, he'd done nothing to reassure her that it wouldn't be for ever. He'd lied by omission, but still it was like a knife to her heart.

'Don't let this come between us,' Tristan pleaded, his voice tight. 'Don't walk away from what we've started to build together, Nina, because I know you feel it too.'

'We both know that this was just a performance,' she whispered.

'It's not,' he growled. 'Not for me, anyway.'

'No, Tristan, I'm not looking for you to placate me or lie for my benefit any more. I know exactly what this deal was when we entered into it. A sham to hold your mother off a little longer. A PR exercise to raise the company's profile with fans. It's just I wasn't expecting to feel so…affected.'

'That's good,' he rasped, taking a step closer.

'Is it?'

'I mean…it's good to know I'm not the only one living in torment.' He reached out to touch her, then paused as if rethinking the movement. 'We spent every single day of the past two weeks together, you in my bed, learning about one another and it still wasn't nearly enough for me. I have absolutely no idea where I stand with you. Yet, my mother took one look at us together and immediately knew the truth.'

'What is the truth?' she asked shakily.

'That I've fallen in love with you, Nina,' he said,

his voice rough, and his eyes trained intently upon her. 'I've fallen in love with everything about you and I want this fake engagement to be real. I love your focus, your ambition, your willingness to fight me at every turn… And of course your body and your ability to drive me wild with just a look.'

Nina's breath caught in her chest; she could hardly believe what she was hearing. 'But the deal, the rules. Your secrets and lies…'

'Forget the rules, forget everything. I thought I was doing the right thing all along, but I think I was only trying to fool myself. I realised in the moment I saw you hit that wall, that nothing I felt for you was simple. I think I fell in love with you that night, holding you in my arms while you monologued about your favourite movies. I'm so sorry I didn't tell you about the company, but I can't go back, Nina…only forwards.'

'You might think you're in love with me, but you barely know me. If you did, you'd never have lied to me.' She shook her head, taking a few steps away. Her heart was hammering in her chest so hard she was surprised she still stood upright but she needed to have this conversation with him. She needed him to understand. 'You've been put under a lot of pressure by your mother to find someone to love. And with your ex getting engaged to your cousin, that had to have hurt you.'

'This isn't about any of that.' He took a step closer, an expression of desperation on his face. 'Look, I can see now that this was a lot to put on you so suddenly. With Alain here, and after learning what I did, maybe

we should wait to talk until later, once you've had time
to think about it.'

'No.' She pulled her hand away from his, and hated
the immediate look of hurt in his eyes. 'Waiting isn't
going to solve any of this, Tristan. We've got so tangled
up in the haze of the past couple weeks I don't know
which way is up any more. I don't know what is real
and what is fake and what is simply induced by spending time with your wonderful yet slightly dramatic family, who I adore.'

'They adore you too,' he said hoarsely.

'Please, stop. I can't think straight with you looking
at me this way.'

'Sometimes thinking straight is the least helpful thing
we can do. Not everything can be made logical and
clear-cut, Nina. Sometimes a person comes storming
into your life when you least expect it, bringing parts
of you back to life that you didn't even realise were
dead. Let's do this for real, let's get married and build
a life together.'

Nina closed her eyes, wishing she could trust this.
Trust *him* after what he'd done. He'd just said he loved
her. She'd dreamed of hearing those words from his
lips. She wished that she could simply take his hands
and throw herself into his arms, throw caution to the
wind. She could just imagine it now: a big white wedding, his entire family would be overjoyed. The media
would love it. A whirlwind romance… Just like the one
she'd grown up as a product of.

Her mother had married her father in the eye of a
media storm, never as happy as when she was the cen-

tre of attention. Every step of their relationship had been scrutinised and followed until her mother had become unrecognisable. Her father had walked away from his marriage and children unscathed, unchanged by the media's opinion, which had largely been aimed at her socialite mother and her supposed sins. Could she do that? Could she trust that whatever this intense connection with Tristan was, she wouldn't be swallowed whole by it?

Her aunt Lola's words rang in her ears.

'Only trust yourself, Nina.'

'I can't,' she whispered, squeezing her eyes tight as if hoping, if she tried hard enough when she opened them, all of this might have just been a bad dream. But it wasn't, and she eventually opened her eyes to see Tristan staring at her as if she were a stranger.

'You can't?' Tristan shook his head. 'Or you won't?'

'I struggle with trusting people, Tristan. I didn't have the same loving family upbringing as you but I know that relationships can be hard to maintain. And if they start out based on lies and deceit—however well meant—what does that say about our future? We've only been together for a short time, and most of that was just for show.'

'It might have started that way, but these past couple of weeks have been real,' he urged. 'Just give us a chance.'

'I can't.' She felt her entire body shake from repressing the tears that threatened to spill from her eyes. 'I'm sorry.'

* * *

Tristan wondered how things could go downhill so quickly. For the past two days he'd been hopeful that Nina might understand why he'd done what he'd done, and had been imagining proposing to her all over again. This time for real. But here she looked at him as though he were a stranger. He should have told her about his deal with her brother sooner, he knew that. But he'd signed that NDA in all good faith, and the longer he'd waited, the deeper the lie had become. And now, seeing the hurt on her face, he wished so hard that he'd done everything differently.

No business deal was worth her pain. Nothing was.

'Even if you had told me the truth right from the start…even if we'd got past all of it, do you really think we would ever have worked as a couple?' Nina closed her eyes, and his chest tightened as he saw a single tear snake from her eyelid down across her cheek. She had never cried in front of him, he realised. She held herself together so tightly, never showing weakness, rarely allowing anybody a glimpse underneath the surface armour to the tender vulnerability beneath.

But over the past few weeks he had slowly dug beneath that armour. She'd *let him in*, damn it—and look how he'd rewarded her trust. Not for the first time since they'd met, he felt like the world's biggest bastard and he reached up with a shaky hand to brush away her tears. She let him touch her, but he knew by the stiffness in her shoulders that it was not an indication of forgiveness. She had told him she struggled to trust, had she not? She had cut people out of her life for far less than this. She burned bridges because it was easier than allowing people a second chance to screw her over again.

'Tell me how to make this right,' he growled, refusing to admit that he had irretrievably broken whatever fragile thing had begun to blossom between them. Refusing to give up on them, even if she was already fading away from his grasp before his eyes.

The silence that stretched between them felt as if it went on for hours, every second ticking down like grains of sand. When she finally spoke, her voice was barely a murmur and her eyes were far away.

'Tristan, this would never have worked out anyway. It was only ever meant to be temporary. Maybe this is what I needed to hear today, to stop feeling this foolish hope.'

'Hope is good,' he rasped, holding himself still as she pulled free from his arms.

'Sometimes hope is just prolonging the pain of something that was always inevitable. We're so different. You're handsome, outgoing and charismatic and I'm…a plain workaholic ice queen.'

She raised her hand to silence him when he immediately rushed to deny her words.

'It's taken me a long time, but I like who I am. I like being obsessed with fast cars and metrics and studying engines until my eyeballs hurt. I like the danger too, Tristan. None of us would be in this career if it didn't give us a thrill. You can barely stand the thought of my job. You flinch every time I mention getting behind the wheel again. Your fears are real and so valid and I feel like—'

He flinched at the hitch in her breath as she paused, shaking her head.

'I feel like if we use hope as the glue to see where this goes, we will only hurt each other very badly in the end. I don't want to hurt you. But is it any better for me to twist myself into smaller pieces, just to keep you comfortable?'

Tristan closed his eyes at the harsh truth in her words. Yes, his fears over her dangerous career were vast and definitely had the potential to pose an issue between them. But was it fair for her to use it as an argument against them together when she hadn't even given them a chance?

'No.' He shook his head. 'I don't accept that, Nina. My fears, while legitimate and a hurdle, are something that I can work on because I would *choose* to work on it for you. That's what you do when you love somebody. You grow, you change, you choose to put eachother first.'

'Maybe I'm just not built that way.'

'We are not born knowing how to trust. It's something you have to learn to do, just like being in love. And I think you *do* love me, but you're angry and afraid to take a chance.'

Her jaw tightened, and her eyes briefly met his. She made no move to refute his words and for one wild moment he thought she might jump into his arms. He prayed she would.

But just as quickly, he seen her shut down once more as she shook her head sadly and looked away towards the deserted racing track.

'Okay,' he said softly, cold seeping into his bones despite the balmy evening air. 'I won't stand here and beg, if you've already made up your mind.'

He felt the last fragile slip of hope slide through his fingers as he took a step backwards and she didn't make a single move to follow him.

CHAPTER FOURTEEN

THE DISTANCE FROM her hotel bed to the bathroom and back was the most movement Nina accomplished over the following two days. With her phone switched off, and a strict do not disturb sign on the door, she ensured herself some peace. At least externally.

Internally however, she was a hurricane of emotion that she couldn't quite separate or work through. She cried silent tears when notes appeared under her door on two separate occasions from Alain. A small package arrived too, a basket filled with her favourite rom-coms and chocolates. No note accompanied the gift, but she knew Tristan had sent it, even before she opened up the simple hotel card to see his sprawling initials on the signature line. She didn't have the appetite for romance or sugar, instead choosing to leave them propped upon the desk in the corner of the room as a reminder. A reminder of what exactly, she wasn't quite sure…why not to trust anyone, perhaps?

Tristan's words rang in her ears.

'We are not born knowing how to trust. It's something you have to learn to do, just like being in love.'

She knew that people made mistakes. She'd made

plenty of mistakes herself in her life. But being lied to and deliberately misled was another thing entirely. Alain had always said she was too rigid in her views, and perhaps she was. She had always been so sensitive to injustice, finding solace in the solid concept of right and wrong. But with her heart broken and her future in the sport she loved uncertain, she just didn't have the energy to make sense of it all. She'd gone from hating Tristan Falco to falling in love with him in a matter of weeks. Surely falling back *out* of love could be achieved simply? Even as she grasped at that thought her chest tightened and her body seemed to push it away. Somehow, she knew that this would not be so easily healed.

She slept for what felt like weeks, the only indication of day bleeding into night coming from a thin slit in the curtains and the glow of the single hotel clock upon her bedstand. It was a slippery slope, allowing her overwhelmed mind to rest this way. She knew from experience that giving in to this kind of exhaustion could lead to a dark place she would only struggle more and more to pick herself back up from.

The next morning, a knock sounded upon the door, one that she did her absolute best to ignore as she burrowed her face deeper and deeper beneath the pillows. Until a familiar voice intruded upon her thoughts.

'You'd better open this door, superstar. Or I'll be calling some hunky Argentinian fireman to chop it down for me.'

Stiff and cranky, Nina forced herself across the room to throw open the door and was practically attacked by the blonde ball of energy that was Sophie. 'You're not supposed to get here until tomorrow.'

'You turn your phone off for *two freaking days* and expect me not to rush here early?' Sophie practically shouted, then she paused and looked around at the chaos of the darkened bedroom. 'It smells like something died in here.'

Perhaps something did… Nina thought mournfully.

'Nope. Stop whatever it is you are thinking right now. I know that face.' Sophie placed her hands on both sides of Nina's cheeks, forcing Nina to look up into her eyes. 'When's the last time you trained?'

Nina shook her head, pulling away to sit down heavily on the side of the bed. 'I'm not driving this weekend; I'm not needed here. I don't know why I don't just go back to Monte Carlo.'

'Dear God, would you listen to yourself? You are a superstar, and superstars need to train. Whatever personal stuff has gone on, it's not worth giving up your career for.'

'What have you heard?' Nina asked roughly.

'Nothing. But I can piece two and two together and get four, darling. I know that whatever has happened, you'll think through it ten times better after running your backside off and cursing at me through your own sweat.'

Nina groaned, pressing her eyelids into her hands. Sophie was right, of course. Her brain craved movement and order to keep regulated. Everything she was feeling was far more intense and unmanageable as a result of her staying here, isolating herself in this room. But she was so tired… So tired of trying so hard all of the time and still ending up right back where she always started. Alone, betrayed.

Sophie kneeled down in front of her, her blue eyes wide and worried and her jaw set in that way Nina knew too well. She was the best trainer in the industry—Falco Roux was not paying her nearly enough. She always knew exactly what to say.

'Okay, thank you for coming to get me.'

'I'll always have your back.' Sophie smiled, leaning in to give her a deep hug. With a polite sniff, she whispered in her ear, 'But I think you need to have a shower first.'

Nina arrived on the morning of race day at the brand-new Argentinian track to find the garage in utter chaos. At least half of the team was missing, and as she wandered around in confusion she spied the team principal, Jock, sitting on the floor with his head in his hands.

'What is it? What happened?' she said, looking frantically around at the worried faces that greeted her.

'They're all dropping like flies, that's what,' he said, running agitated hands through the little hair he had remaining upon his head.

Sophie appeared at her side, a worried frown creasing her forehead. 'They went out to eat at a restaurant last night, with Daniele Roberts. At least a quarter of the team have food poisoning. Some of them have gone to hospital. Including Roberts.'

'Oh, God, is he going to be okay?' She felt her heart drop. 'How bad is it?'

'We're not sure quite how bad it is yet, but with food

poisoning he's bound to be out for a couple of days at least. Even then, his recovery could be slow.'

'We are *screwed*,' the team principal growled. 'I'm down five mechanics, we have backups on the way, but who knows what kind of speed they're going to be? I can't believe this. We were so close to winning the constructors' championship.'

'It will be okay. I'm good to step in as reserve.' Nina's mind worked furiously over the statistics and strategies they'd perfected recently. Their new star was good, but Apollo was still settling in. If he made a mistake in the first seat and didn't secure a third-place finish at the minimum, they'd lose the constructors' championship. If Nina took first seat and drove her very best…they still had a chance. But as she opened her mouth and began relaying her thoughts, the older man immediately scoffed.

'After that stunt you pulled in Spain? There's not a chance I'd put my faith in you, Roux. You lack the aggression required to drive in first. I won't clear it.'

His phone rang and he growled, taking the call and walking away.

Apollo was already suited up and preparing for the first practice session when Nina walked into the opposite end of the garage.

'Looks like you're driving with me, Roux,' he said, a brief attempt at a smile on his handsome face.

'I won't clear it, Falco.' The team principal appeared, still bellowing into his phone. His face sweaty and red. 'You think you can just call me up and demand I put your fiancée in my first seat? I'd rather walk.'

Nina frowned. Tristan? That was who was on the call?

'I mean it, Falco,' Jock cried. 'I'll leave.'

Whatever Tristan's reply was, the older man's face blanched and he threw his phone down on the ground with a growl, smashing the device to pieces.

'I support the decision to seat Nina first,' Apollo said matter-of-factly. 'We won't have to argue about it then.'

'You actually agree with that madman?' Jock bellowed. 'In my thirty years at this team, I have never heard such ridiculous—'

'I'd stop right there or you'll be fired, Jock.' Alain appeared behind them. 'Then we'll be down a team principal today as well as half our team.'

'Alain! I wasn't aware that you were back. Good, I might get you to talk some sense into that man who took over our team.'

Alain moved to stand behind Nina, his hand upon her shoulder. 'I think you'll find that it's *our* team. As of today, our shares have been restored to us by Tristan Falco and I've been appointed as managing director once again. Myself and my sister have not agreed on many things, but the fact that she is the most qualified person here to lead this team today is not one that's up for debate.'

'Thank you, Alain,' Nina said, a lump in her throat. 'I know our contracts stated that Apollo was to be in first, and most of my experience so far has been in second...'

'You can do it,' Apollo said encouragingly. 'Even with my experience, we all know it was the plan for me to drive in second seat today, Nina. I've seen you instruct our strategy team on how to help Roberts win; you are undoubtedly the natural choice for first driver today.'

'Seems like you're getting your way again, *princess*.' Jock glowered.

'You know what? I've had enough of you,' Nina growled. 'If it's true that my shares are back…then I've been waiting a long time to say these words. Jock, you're fired.'

Nina's eyes widened as the team principal lunged towards her and her brother launched to her defence before shouting for security to remove the abusive old bat from the garage once and for all.

In the chaos that followed, Alain announced that he was going to be acting team principal for the day, a position that he'd hoped to wait until next season to assume after undergoing training while at the recovery centre. He didn't need training, of course, he'd grown up on the track just as she had. He'd never shown any aptitude for the driving side of things, but he had always had a way with people. She looked at him, seeing once again how vibrant and alive he looked, and she realised belatedly that she had Tristan to thank for all of it.

Tristan, the man who had allowed the world to paint him as a frivolous playboy, swiping up a team in a sport he had no knowledge of or interest in simply to avoid the destruction of a long-respected Elite One racing team. When all the while, he had actually been their saviour. Yes, he'd made mistakes along the way. But didn't everyone?

Closing her eyes, she leaned her head down upon a stack of tyres and took a deep breath, hoping and praying that all of her training would stand up as she attempted to pull off what was the most difficult feat of her entire career.

As she drove into her starting position on the grid, she looked up to the box where she hoped Tristan would be, even though he had no reason to stay for today's race. He'd done his part in launching the event and had participated in countless press calls. Now that the end of his role as team owner had arrived he could slip away without anyone knowing any differently.

As her eyes scanned the crowd of guests in the box, she felt her chest tighten with relief. He'd stayed. He stood head and shoulders above everyone else, his handsome features looking pinched and drawn. He was still here, standing guard in his brooding fallen-angel way, silently supporting her even after she'd rejected him and walked away.

She knew family wasn't supposed to give up on you, unlike her parents. Her aunt Lola had always said love meant always being there, even if you were fighting, even when you messed up. Real love was unconditional. She had never known that kind of love, she hadn't known how to accept it when he'd so bravely tried to make her see what he was offering to her.

But now…she wanted to try.

CHAPTER FIFTEEN

SHE'D DONE IT.

Tristan almost burst with pride as he watched Nina take her third place upon the podium. The first podium of her career in Elite One and, judging by the calibre of her driving today, it would not be the last.

As well as winning third place, their team had scaled their win of the constructors' championship. Alain, looking awkward as ever, had to take the stage to accept the trophy for Falco Roux, which he did with an emotional cheer coming from the crowd. Tristan felt a maelstrom of emotion as he watched the siblings embrace, and he knew that if this was the only good thing that had come from his involvement in their lives, it would be enough.

He had been the one to suggest that Alain stepped back into management early now that he was well. But still, it hurt to know that he would not be the one to congratulate the woman he loved in person today. He was content to stand back and allow her to shine, enjoying the moment she'd thoroughly earned. She had an entire crowd of screaming fans waiting for her, press and experts all waiting to dissect her drive and hear her speak about the sport she was a true expert in. She was a superstar, and he was glad that the world was finally seeing it too.

Perhaps it was cowardly, but he had only intended to stay long enough to see her take her place on that podium. Now that it was done, he needed to get away.

Walking away from the crowd, he took a shortcut through the long corridor that led behind the garages, unable to resist taking one last look into the world she'd shown him and made him fall for too. The Falco Roux garage was still lit up, rows upon rows of tyres and instruments shining in disarray as they'd all been dropped in the midst of their celebrations. He would never be near the scent of engine oil and not think of Nina Roux.

Sounds behind him caught his attention and he turned to see a familiar figure in the doorway. Her red racing suit was covered in liquid as though she'd been in heavy rain, her hair wet with celebratory champagne and plastered to her face. But the look in her eyes was what made him pause.

'You didn't leave.' She breathed heavily, as though she'd been running.

'I came to watch you race. I couldn't stay away. You're amazing and I can't believe I ever signed Apollo instead of you. Is that the only reason you chased me down here?'

'I didn't chase…' she began, and then shook her head. 'No, I told myself I wasn't going to fight you. I told myself it was time to be brave.'

'You're always brave,' he said huskily.

'Am I? Because you told me that you loved me and you told me that when you love someone, you grow and you change, and you choose to put eachother first. But I did the opposite of all that. I ran from your love. I was the coward.'

He dared to hope that what he was hearing was exactly what he thought it was, that she'd finally realised she could trust him with her heart. That he would always be there for her. But still he remained in place, not daring to touch her until he knew for sure. 'What are you saying, exactly, Nina?'

'I'm saying, I'm hopelessly in love with you, Tristan Falco. I couldn't stop loving you if I tried.'

Nina felt as though her heart were about to beat out of her chest as Tristan remained silent, his feet still planted firmly in the centre of the garage where he remained frozen in place. She had seen him in the crowd as she'd accepted her third-place trophy and as the traditional champagne bottles had been popped and sprayed around the place. It was a moment she had waited for her entire life and yet all she'd been able to think of was running to him. Not having Tristan in her life was like missing a limb.

'You love me?' he repeated.

'I love you so much,' she declared, allowing all of the emotion she felt to bleed into her voice without fear. She was done being afraid. 'I want a future with you, Tristan, or at the very least I want the hope of one. I want to be yours and I want you to be mine, if you'll still have me. You were right, love is about changing and growing and you make me want to grow. You see me and you make me want to be a better version of myself.'

He moved towards her in a flurry of motion, or perhaps she moved towards him. It all became a blur as they fell into one another's arms, mouths meeting in a riot of heat and relief and love… So much love.

After she was pretty sure all of the breath had been pulled from her lungs and her heart grew a couple of sizes once more, she pulled back and met his eyes.

'Do you forgive me for rejecting you and walking away?' she asked.

'Only if you forgive me for being an impossible fool. I tried to do my best to make good on everything, by encouraging Alain to take back control and returning the shares. But I know it's not enough. I should have told you the truth from the start.'

'It's enough,' she breathed, placing another kiss on his lips. 'You are enough, Tristan, more than enough. Too much really, by most people's standards, but I accept you just as you are. Flamboyant dress sense and all.'

'Perhaps my dress sense will rub off on you?' he teased. 'I won't lose hope just yet.'

'Let's not go that far, darling.' An idea occurring to her, Nina took a step back and looked around the floor. Finding exactly what she wanted, she smirked and dropped to one knee before him.

'What are you doing now?' He smiled, then froze as he realised what she held in her hand.

'I never want to wake up in a world where you're not by my side so… I guess I'm actually more traditional than I thought?' With an oversized wheel nut, Nina proposed to the man she loved.

It wasn't quite the rare black diamond that he had

presented her with all those weeks ago, but it felt right. Just as it felt right when he lifted her up into his arms, shouting his acceptance as he twirled her in a circle.

'We're going to have to negotiate some new terms for our engagement, real ones this time,' Nina joked.

'No wedding until you win a driver's championship,' Tristan suggested.

'I accept.' She laughed. 'And no babies until I've won three.'

Tristan's eyes darkened, his hands pulling her closer as he breathed in her scent. 'Did you just tell me you want to have my babies, Nina Roux? Dear God... I'm barely keeping my hands off you as it is.'

'I do... But not for a while yet. I want to enjoy you all to myself for as long as I can.'

'It's okay, I'm not ready to hang up my playboy hat just yet either.' He laughed as her expression immediately turned incredulous. 'I mean that I have a new routine to perfect now. To prepare for. The playboy husband experience.'

'What exactly does a playboy husband do?' Nina asked breathlessly as her fiancé's lips began to wander scandalously low on her chest, and he unzipped her racing suit inch by inch as he lowered himself to his knees.

'He is scandalous, dissolute, utterly shocking,' he murmured against her belly button. 'He also seduces his wife in very inappropriate places.'

Nina smiled. 'Thank goodness for that.'

More passionate kissing ensued, and they might or might not have consummated their engagement up against a stack of tyres in the dark. To all intents and purposes it was the most romantic thing Nina could have ever hoped for. The perfect place for them to pledge their love to one another permanently.

EPILOGUE

NINA STARED AT her reflection in the floor-length mirror of the church vestry and fought the urge to smile. It was her wedding day, and not only was she excitedly awaiting the prospect of getting married... She was wearing white.

She hadn't set out for a traditional look when Tristan's mama had accompanied her shopping in Buenos Aires just two days ago when Tristan had finally agreed to elope with her. Well, he'd half agreed—hence why she presently stood in a church and not in a tiny Las Vegas chapel as she'd suggested.

She smiled to herself, remembering the exultant look on his face when she'd stepped down off her podium after winning her very first world championship right here at the Falco Aerodrome and immediately reminded him of the deal they'd made upon their official engagement four years before. He'd swung her around in a circle while the crowd whooped and cheered, unaware that they were witnessing the final taming of Argentina's wildest playboy. Today, they would become husband and wife in the same church where his mother had said her loving vows to Tristan's father and Agustin. Nothing in her life had ever felt more right than it did at this moment.

Tristan's mother stood nearby, fussing over a delicate lace veil and deftly securing it to a pair of discreet combs with her bejewelled hands. Dulce had asked if she would wear the veil she had worn on her wedding day to Tristan's father.

'I've been instructed to wait until this moment to give you another surprise from my son.' The woman's eyes sparkled with mischief, so like the charming rake she had raised.

'What on earth has he planned now?' Nina smiled wryly, watching with only a little trepidation as Dulce moved to retrieve a slim square box from her bag. The box was emblazoned with the Falco crown, the symbol that Tristan had brought back to glory as a worldwide status symbol as he worked tirelessly on various campaigns over the past few years.

'He said that you would understand, once you saw it.'

Nina held her breath as the box was opened and felt a wide smile take over her face as a familiar gold and sapphire tiara was revealed. The same tiara that she had worn on the night they had first officially met. The night that everything in her life had changed…and she had been utterly swept up in the storm that was Tristan Falco.

Her throat tightened with emotion as she helped Dulce position the delicate piece upon her head and watched with a sense of surreal awe as one of the world's greatest fashion icons primped and fussed with her veil until she was satisfied.

'Stunning,' Dulce whispered, placing a single kiss upon her cheek before quietly exiting to give Nina a few more moments alone. It didn't last very long however, as another knock sounded, this time Alain arriving to tell her that it was time to go.

She linked her arm through her brother's, breathing a deep sigh of relief that he had agreed to walk her down the aisle today, in lieu of her father. Neither of her parents had bothered to come. But she still had Alain in her life. He'd supported her when she chose to speak publicly about her experience of late-diagnosed autism the year before, just as she'd supported him when he decided to seek treatment for ADHD. They laughed as they walked and Alain made quiet jokes under his breath like he used to do when they were kids, trying to make her laugh, trying to make her break the character of the good society girl.

And she did laugh, without any worry of what the high-society Argentinian guests might think of their beloved playboy's unconventional bride. Because the moment her groom turned and his eyes met hers she knew that there could be nothing more right in this world.

Of all the people that Tristan Falco had imagined giving a speech on his wedding day, Alain Roux was not one of them. And yet here they were, grand tables filling the courtyard of his family's historic estate as Nina's brother recounted a mildly embarrassing story about the bride and groom in his usual entertaining style before wishing the new Mr and Mrs Falco health and happiness.

Tristan leaned across to kiss his wife while applause

erupted around them and once again he felt an over-whelming urge to gather her into his arms and steal her away. Watching her walk down the aisle towards him had been overwhelming, but that was nothing compared to the feeling of finally sliding a wedding band onto her finger after four long years of waiting. She'd been worth every second.

When they stood up for their first dance, Nina had a mischievous sparkle in her eye. As he led her onto the dance floor he leaned down to whisper in her ear, 'I know that look, what on earth are you up to?'

'You're not the only one who has surprises up their sleeve,' she murmured before spinning herself out into a circle on the floor as the low hum of an Argentine tango sounded out from the band.

Tristan watched with wide eyes as his sultry wife clipped off the skirt of her wedding gown to reveal a more slim-fitting knee-length skirt beneath. She raised a brow in his direction before clapping her hands and beginning the slow sequence of moves that led the dance. The moves she had performed when he had tried to teach her all those years ago, much to the entertainment of their guests. It seemed she had been secretly taking lessons. His stomach tightened as he watched her sensual movements. She was quite literally dancing circles around him while he watched. It took a moment to remember that he was supposed to respond in the dance, and so he did, moving in and allowing her to lead him. After a few moments, Nina stepped in and murmured in his ear, 'Your turn.'

She bent at the waist, reaching her hand towards him

for him to lead her this time. It was a beautiful reflection of their marriage, he realised. All the ebb and flow of the partnership they had built together over the past four years as he had supported her in her bid to become the first female Elite One champion. He had never been more proud than in the moment he had watched her lift that trophy high above her head, her eyes meeting his with triumph.

Now, as the dance came to an end and she spun into his arms, her body flush against his chest, he knew that he would always support her, no matter what she wanted to achieve. They championed one another, him supporting her and her doing the same for him as he'd brought his mother's company back to its former glory. Their relationship itself was a dance, an invigorating sequence of moves in tandem as they led one another to be the best version of themselves.

When all their guests had finally left, Tristan and Nina stayed in the dark of the courtyard hand in hand, looking up at the stars.

'What next?' She laughed, her head leaning back into his chest. 'We've done the championship and you've taken the fashion world by storm. Not to mention you finally nabbed me as your wife.'

'I nabbed you, did I?'

'Well, I suppose technically I'm the one who tamed the world's most untameable playboy, aren't I? But I suppose… Things might get a little boring around here if we don't up the challenges a little.'

'*Querida*, you couldn't bore me if you tried.'

'Tristan, I'm trying to tell you that I'm ready.'

Her meaning took a moment to sink in, and he frowned, looking down into her beautiful face. 'You're ready... For the next step?'

She knew he wanted children, and when she'd proposed to him she'd told him she wanted to win the championship three times first before becoming a mother. But...

'I've decided to take next season off to focus on growing the girls academy. And while I have some downtime... I think we could start our family. I find myself quite impatient to have your babies, Tristan Falco.'

'Dear God... That sentence from your lips... You're going to give me a heart attack right here and we've only been married a few hours.'

'So dramatic. I have conditions, of course.'

'Ah, I should have guessed that this would be a contract negotiation.'

'I have my terms... We have to practise quite a lot first, so that I know you're up to the job.'

'Oh, I'm up to the job, I assure you. So I propose that we begin today, this exact moment, in fact.'

She laughed as he chased her inside, into their bedroom, spinning her until she fell backwards onto the bed and he proceeded to make good on that threat, proving once again that he was the best adventure she'd ever taken a chance on.

* * * * *

If Fast-Track Fiancé *left you wanting more,*
then make sure you catch up on the first instalment of
The Fast-Track Billionaires' Club trilogy
The Bump in Their Forbidden Reunion

And why not explore these other
Amanda Cinelli stories?

The Vows He Must Keep
Returning to Claim His Heir
Stolen in Her Wedding Gown
The Billionaire's Last-Minute Marriage
Pregnant in the Italian's Palazzo

Available now!

HARLEQUIN
Reader Service

Enjoyed your book?

Try the perfect subscription for Romance readers and get more great books like this delivered right to your door.

See why over 10+ million readers have tried Harlequin Reader Service.

Start with a Free Welcome Collection with free books and a gift—valued over $20.

Choose any series in print or ebook. See website for details and order today:

   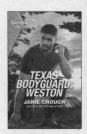

TryReaderService.com/subscriptions